The Silver Chair

BOOK ONE

The Magician's Nephew

BOOK TWO

The Lion, the Witch and the Wardrobe

BOOK THREE

The Horse and His Boy

BOOK FOUR

Prince Caspian

BOOK FIVE

The Voyage of the Dawn Treader

BOOK SIX

The Silver Chair

BOOK SEVEN

The Last Battle

C. S. Lewis.

The Silver Chair

BOOK SIX

The Chronicles of Narnia

HARPERCOLLINSPUBLISHERS

NARNIA®

Although *The Magician's Nephew* was written several years after C. S. Lewis first began The Chronicles of Narnia®, he wanted it to be read as the first book in the series. HarperCollins is happy to present these books in the order in which Professor Lewis preferred.

The Chronicles of Narnia®, Narnia® and all book titles, characters and locales original to The Chronicles of Narnia are trademarks of C.S. Lewis Pte. Ltd. Use without permission is strictly prohibited.

Library of Congress Catalog Card Number: 2004113555

ISBN 0-06-076493-7

Typography by Karin Paprocki

❖

To Nicholas Hardie

Contents

One   Behind the Gym   1

Two   Jill Is Given a Task   17

Three   The Sailing of the King   33

Four   A Parliament of Owls   50

Five   Puddleglum   67

Six   The Wild Waste Lands of the North   83

Seven   The Hill of the Strange Trenches   101

Eight   The House of Harfang   118

Nine   How They Discovered Something
           Worth Knowing   135

Ten   Travels Without the Sun   151

Eleven   In the Dark Castle   168

Twelve	The Queen of Underland	184
Thirteen	Underland Without the Queen	201
Fourteen	The Bottom of the World	217
Fifteen	The Disappearance of Jill	233
Sixteen	The Healing of Harms	249

The Silver Chair

Chapter One

Behind the Gym

IT WAS A DULL AUTUMN DAY AND JILL POLE WAS crying behind the gym.

She was crying because they had been bullying her. This is not going to be a school story, so I shall say as little as possible about Jill's school, which is not a pleasant subject. It was "Co-educational," a school for both boys and girls, what used to be called a "mixed" school; some said it was not nearly so mixed as the minds of the people who ran it. These people had the idea that boys and girls should be allowed to do what they liked. And unfortunately what ten or fifteen of the biggest boys and girls liked best was bullying the others. All sorts of things, horrid things, went on which at an ordinary school would have been found out and stopped in half a term; but at this school they weren't. Or even if they were, the people who did them were not expelled or punished. The Head said they were interesting psychological cases and sent for them and talked to them for hours. And if you knew the right sort of things to say to the Head, the main result was that you became rather a favorite than otherwise.

That was why Jill Pole was crying on that dull autumn day on the damp little path which runs between the back of the gym and the shrubbery. And she hadn't nearly finished her cry when a boy came round the corner of the gym whistling, with his hands in his pockets. He nearly ran into her.

"Can't you look where you're going?" said Jill Pole.

"All *right*," said the boy, "you needn't start—" and then he noticed her face. "I say, Pole," he said, "what's up?"

Jill only made faces; the sort you make when you're

trying to say something but find that if you speak you'll start crying again.

"It's *Them*, I suppose—as usual," said the boy grimly, digging his hands farther into his pockets.

Jill nodded. There was no need for her to say anything, even if she could have said it. They both knew.

"Now, look here," said the boy, "there's no good us all—"

He meant well, but he *did* talk rather like someone beginning a lecture. Jill suddenly flew into a temper (which is quite a likely thing to happen if you have been interrupted in a cry).

"Oh, go away and mind your own business," she said. "Nobody asked you to come barging in, did they? And you're a nice person to start telling us what we all ought to do, aren't you? I suppose you mean we ought to spend all our time sucking up to Them, and currying favor, and dancing attendance on Them like you do."

"Oh, Lor!" said the boy, sitting down on the grassy bank at the edge of the shrubbery and very quickly getting up again because the grass was soaking wet. His name unfortunately was Eustace Scrubb, but he wasn't a bad sort.

"Pole!" he said. "Is that fair? Have I been doing anything of the sort this term? Didn't I stand up to Carter about the rabbit? And didn't I keep the secret about Spivvins—under torture too? And didn't I—"

"I d-don't know and I don't care," sobbed Jill.

Scrubb saw that she wasn't quite herself yet and very sensibly offered her a peppermint. He had one too. Presently Jill began to see things in a clearer light.

"I'm sorry, Scrubb," she said presently. "I wasn't fair. You have done all that—this term."

"Then wash out last term if you can," said Eustace. "I was a different chap then. I was—gosh! what a little tick I was."

"Well, honestly, you were," said Jill.

"You think there has been a change, then?" said Eustace.

"It's not only me," said Jill. "Everyone's been saying so. *They*'ve noticed it. Eleanor Blakiston heard Adela Pennyfather talking about it in our changing room yesterday. She said, 'Someone's got hold of that Scrubb kid. He's quite unmanageable this term. We shall have to attend to *him* next.'"

Eustace gave a shudder. Everyone at Experiment House knew what it was like being "attended to" by *Them*.

Both children were quiet for a moment. The drops dripped off the laurel leaves.

"Why were you so different last term?" said Jill presently.

"A lot of queer things happened to me in the hols," said Eustace mysteriously.

"What sort of things?" asked Jill.

Eustace didn't say anything for quite a long time. Then he said:

"Look here, Pole, you and I hate this place about as much as anybody can hate anything, don't we?"

"I know I do," said Jill.

"Then I really think I can trust you."

"Dam' good of you," said Jill.

"Yes, but this is a really terrific secret. Pole, I say, are you good at believing things? I mean things that everyone here would laugh at?"

"I've never had the chance," said Jill, "but I think I would be."

"Could you believe me if I said I'd been right out of the world—outside this world—last hols?"

"I wouldn't know what you meant."

"Well, don't let's bother about worlds then. Supposing I told you I'd been in a place where animals can talk and where there are—er—enchantments and dragons—and—well, all the sorts of things you have in fairy-tales." Scrubb felt terribly awkward as he said this and got red in the face.

"How did you get there?" said Jill. She also felt curiously shy.

"The only way you can—by Magic," said Eustace almost in a whisper. "I was with two cousins of mine. We were just—whisked away. They'd been there before."

Now that they were talking in whispers Jill somehow felt it easier to believe. Then suddenly a horrible suspicion came over her and she said (so fiercely that for the moment she looked like a tigress):

"If I find you've been pulling my leg I'll never speak to you again; never, never, never."

"I'm not," said Eustace. "I swear I'm not. I swear by—by everything."

(When I was at school one would have said, "I swear by the Bible." But Bibles were not encouraged at Experiment House.)

"All right," said Jill, "I'll believe you."

"And tell nobody?"

"What do you take me for?"

They were very excited as they said this. But when they had said it and Jill looked round and saw the dull autumn sky and heard the drip off the leaves and thought of all the hopelessness of Experiment House (it was a thirteen-week term and there were still eleven weeks to come) she said:

"But after all, what's the good? We're not there: we're here. And we jolly well can't get *there*. Or can we?"

"That's what I've been wondering," said Eustace. "When we came back from That Place, Someone said that the two Pevensie kids (that's my two cousins) could never go there again. It was their third time, you see. I suppose they've had their share. But he never said I couldn't. Surely he would have said so, unless he meant that I was to get back? And I can't help wondering, can we—could we—?"

"Do you mean, do something to make it happen?"

Eustace nodded.

"You mean we might draw a circle on the ground—and write in queer letters in it—and stand inside it—and recite charms and spells?"

"Well," said Eustace after he had thought hard for a bit. "I believe that was the sort of thing I was thinking of, though I never did it. But now that it comes to the point, I've an idea that all those circles and things are rather rot. I don't think he'd like them. It would look as if we thought we could make him do things. But really, we can only ask him."

"Who is this person you keep on talking about?"

"They call him Aslan in That Place," said Eustace.

"What a curious name!"

"Not half so curious as himself," said Eustace solemnly. "But let's get on. It can't do any harm, just asking. Let's stand side by side, like this. And we'll hold out our arms in front of us with the palms down: like they did in Ramandu's Island—"

"Whose island?"

"I'll tell you about that another time. And he might like us to face the east. Let's see, where is the east?"

"I don't know," said Jill.

"It's an extraordinary thing about girls that they never know the points of the compass," said Eustace.

"You don't know either," said Jill indignantly.

"Yes I do, if only you didn't keep on interrupting. I've got it now. That's the east, facing up into the laurels. Now, will you say the words after me?"

"What words?" asked Jill.

"The words I'm going to say, of course," answered Eustace. "Now—"

And he began, "Aslan, Aslan, Aslan!"

"Aslan, Aslan, Aslan," repeated Jill.

"Please let us two go into—"

At that moment a voice from the other side of the gym was heard shouting out, "Pole? Yes. I know where she is. She's blubbing behind the gym. Shall I fetch her out?"

Jill and Eustace gave one glance at each other, dived under the laurels, and began scrambling up the steep, earthy slope of the shrubbery at a speed which did them great credit. (Owing to the curious methods of teaching at Experiment House, one did not learn much French or

Maths or Latin or things of that sort; but one did learn a
lot about getting away quickly and quietly when They
were looking for one.)

   After about a minute's scramble they stopped to listen,
and knew by the noises they heard that they were being
followed.

   "If only the door was open again!" said Scrubb as they
went on, and Jill nodded. For at the top of the shrubbery
was a high stone wall and in that wall a door by which you
could get out on to open moor. This door was nearly
always locked. But there had been times when people had
found it open; or perhaps there had been only one time.
But you may imagine how the memory of even one time
kept people hoping, and trying the door; for if it should
happen to be unlocked it would be a splendid way of getting outside the school grounds without being seen.

   Jill and Eustace, now both very hot and very grubby
from going along bent almost double under the laurels,
panted up to the wall. And there was the door, shut as usual.

   "It's sure to be no good," said Eustace with his hand on
the handle; and then, "O-o-oh. By Gum!!" For the handle

turned and the door opened.

A moment before, both of them had meant to get through that doorway in double quick time, if by any chance the door was not locked. But when the door actually opened, they both stood stock still. For what they saw was quite different from what they had expected.

They had expected to see the gray, heathery slope of the moor going up and up to join the dull autumn sky. Instead, a blaze of sunshine met them. It poured through the doorway as the light of a June day pours into a garage when you open the door. It made the drops of water on the grass glitter like beads and showed up the dirtiness of Jill's tear-stained face. And the sunlight was coming from what certainly did look like a different world—what they could see of it. They saw smooth turf, smoother and brighter than Jill had ever seen before, and blue sky, and, darting to and fro, things so bright that they might have been jewels or huge butterflies.

Although she had been longing for something like this, Jill felt frightened. She looked at Scrubb's face and saw that he was frightened too.

"Come on, Pole," he said in a breathless voice.

"Can we get back? Is it safe?" asked Jill.

At that moment a voice shouted from behind, a mean, spiteful little voice. "Now then, Pole," it squeaked. "Everyone knows you're there. Down you come." It was the voice of Edith Jackle, not one of Them herself but one of their hangers-on and tale-bearers.

"Quick!" said Scrubb. "Here. Hold hands. We mustn't get separated." And before she quite knew what was happening, he had grabbed her hand and pulled her through the door, out of the school grounds, out of England, out of our whole world into That Place.

The sound of Edith Jackle's voice stopped as suddenly as the voice on the radio when it is switched off. Instantly there was a quite different sound all about them. It came from those bright things overhead, which now turned out to be birds. They were making a riotous noise, but it was much more like music—rather advanced music which you don't quite take in at the first hearing—than birds' songs ever are in our world. Yet, in spite of the singing, there was a sort of background of immense silence. That silence, combined with the freshness of the air, made Jill think they must be on the top of a very high mountain.

Scrubb still had her by the hand and they were walking forward, staring about them on every side. Jill saw that huge trees, rather like cedars but bigger, grew in every direction. But as they did not grow close together, and as there was no undergrowth, this did not prevent one from seeing a long way into the forest to left and right. And as far as Jill's eye could reach, it was all the same—level turf, darting birds with yellow, or dragonfly blue, or rainbow plumage, blue shadows, and emptiness. There was not a breath of wind in that cool, bright air. It was a very lonely forest.

Right ahead there were no trees: only blue sky. They went straight on without speaking till suddenly Jill heard Scrubb say, "Look out!" and felt herself jerked back. They were at the very edge of a cliff.

Jill was one of those lucky people who have a good head for heights. She didn't mind in the least standing on the edge of a precipice. She was rather annoyed with Scrubb for pulling her back—"just as if I was a kid," she said—and she wrenched her hand out of his. When she saw how very white he had turned, she despised him.

"What's the matter?" she said. And to show that she was not afraid, she stood very near the edge indeed; in fact, a good deal nearer than even she liked. Then she looked down.

She now realized that Scrubb had some excuse for looking white, for no cliff in our world is to be compared with this. Imagine yourself at the top of the very highest cliff you know. And imagine yourself looking down to the very bottom. And then imagine that the precipice goes on below that, as far again, ten times as far, twenty times as far. And when you've looked down all that distance imagine little white things that might, at first glance, be mistaken for sheep, but presently you realize that they are clouds— not little wreaths of mist but the enormous white, puffy clouds which are themselves as big as most mountains. And at last, in between those clouds, you get your first glimpse of the real bottom, so far away that you can't make out whether it's field or wood, or land or water: farther below those clouds than you are above them.

Jill stared at it. Then she thought that perhaps, after all, she would step back a foot or so from the edge; but she didn't like to for fear of what Scrubb would think. Then she suddenly decided that she didn't care what he thought, and that she would jolly well get away from that horrible edge and never laugh at anyone for not liking heights again. But when she tried to move, she found she couldn't. Her legs seemed to have turned into putty. Everything was swimming before her eyes.

"What are you doing, Pole? Come back—blithering little idiot!" shouted Scrubb. But his voice seemed to be coming from a long way off. She felt him grabbing at her. But by now she had no control over her own arms and legs. There was a moment's struggling on the cliff edge. Jill was too frightened and dizzy to know quite what she was doing, but two things she remembered as long as she lived (they often came back to her in dreams). One was that she had wrenched herself free of Scrubb's clutches; the other was that, at the same moment, Scrubb himself, with a terrified scream, had lost his balance and gone hurtling to the depths.

Fortunately, she was given no time to think over what she had done. Some huge, brightly colored animal had rushed to the edge of the cliff. It was lying down, leaning over; and (this was the odd thing) blowing. Not roaring or snorting, but just blowing from its wide-opened mouth; blowing out as steadily as a vacuum cleaner sucks in. Jill was lying so close to the creature that she could feel the breath vibrating steadily through its body. She was lying still because she couldn't get up. She was nearly fainting: indeed, she wished she could really faint, but faints don't come for the asking. At last she saw, far away below her, a tiny black speck floating away from the cliff and slightly upward. As it rose, it also got farther away. By the time it was nearly on a level with the cliff-top it was so far off that she lost sight of it. It was obviously moving away from them at a great speed. Jill couldn't help thinking that the creature at her side was blowing it away.

So she turned and looked at the creature. It was a lion.

Chapter Two

Jill Is Given a Task

WITHOUT A GLANCE AT JILL THE LION ROSE TO ITS feet and gave one last blow. Then, as if satisfied with its work, it turned and stalked slowly away, back into the forest.

"It must be a dream, it must, it must," said Jill to herself. "I'll wake up in a moment." But it wasn't, and she didn't.

"I do wish we'd never come to this dreadful place," said Jill. "I don't believe Scrubb knew any more about it than I do. Or if he did, he had no business to bring me here without warning me what it was like. It's not my fault he fell over that cliff. If he'd left me alone we should both be all right." Then she remembered again the scream that Scrubb had given when he fell, and burst into tears.

Crying is all right in its way while it lasts. But you have to stop sooner or later, and then you still have to decide what to do. When Jill stopped, she found she was dreadfully thirsty. She had been lying face downward, and now she sat up. The birds had ceased singing and there was perfect silence except for one small, persistent sound, which seemed to come from a good distance away. She listened carefully, and felt almost sure it was the sound of running water.

Jill got up and looked round her very carefully. There was no sign of the lion; but there were so many trees about that it might easily be quite close without her seeing it. For all she knew, there might be several lions. But her thirst was very bad now, and she plucked up her courage to go and look for that running water. She went on tiptoes, stealing cautiously from tree to tree, and stopping to peer round her at every step.

The wood was so still that it was not difficult to decide where the sound was coming from. It grew clearer every moment and, sooner than she expected, she came to an open glade and saw the stream, bright as glass, running across the turf a stone's throw away from her. But although the sight of the water made her feel ten times thirstier than before, she didn't rush forward and drink. She stood as still as if she had been turned into stone, with her mouth wide open. And she had a very good reason; just on this side of the stream lay the lion.

It lay with its head raised and its two fore-paws out in front of it, like the lions in Trafalgar Square. She knew at once that it had seen her, for its eyes looked straight into hers for a moment and then turned away—as if it knew her quite well and didn't think much of her.

"If I run away, it'll be after me in a moment," thought Jill. "And if I go on, I shall run straight into its mouth." Anyway, she couldn't have moved if she had tried, and she couldn't take her eyes off it. How long this lasted, she could not be sure; it seemed like hours. And the thirst became so bad that she almost felt she would not mind being eaten by the lion if only she could be sure of getting a mouthful of water first.

"If you're thirsty, you may drink."

They were the first words she had heard since Scrubb had spoken to her on the edge of the cliff. For a second she stared here and there, wondering who had spoken. Then the voice said again, "If you are thirsty, come and drink," and of course she remembered what Scrubb had said about animals talking in that other world, and realized that it was the lion speaking. Anyway, she had seen its lips move this time, and the voice was not like a man's. It was deeper, wilder, and stronger; a sort of heavy, golden voice. It did not make her any less frightened than she had been before, but it made her frightened in rather a different way.

"Are you not thirsty?" said the Lion.

"I'm *dying* of thirst," said Jill.

"Then drink," said the Lion.

"May I—could I—would you mind going away while I do?" said Jill.

The Lion answered this only by a look and a very low growl. And as Jill gazed at its motionless bulk, she realized that she might as well have asked the whole mountain to move aside for her convenience.

The delicious rippling noise of the stream was driving her nearly frantic.

"Will you promise not to—do anything to me, if I do come?" said Jill.

"I make no promise," said the Lion.

Jill was so thirsty now that, without noticing it, she had come a step nearer.

"*Do* you eat girls?" she said.

"I have swallowed up girls and boys, women and men, kings and emperors, cities and realms," said the Lion. It didn't say this as if it were boasting, nor as if it were sorry, nor as if it were angry. It just said it.

"I daren't come and drink," said Jill.

"Then you will die of thirst," said the Lion.

"Oh dear!" said Jill, coming another step nearer. "I suppose I must go and look for another stream then."

"There is no other stream," said the Lion.

It never occurred to Jill to disbelieve the Lion—no one who had seen his stern face could do that—and her mind suddenly made itself up. It was the worst thing she had ever had to do, but she went forward to the stream, knelt down, and began scooping up water in her hand. It was the coldest, most refreshing water she had ever tasted. You didn't need to drink much of it, for it quenched your thirst at once. Before she tasted it she had been intending to make a dash away from the Lion the moment she had finished. Now, she realized that this would be on the whole the most dangerous thing of all. She got up and stood there with her lips still wet from drinking.

"Come here," said the Lion. And she had to. She was almost between its front paws now, looking straight into its face. But she couldn't stand that for long; she dropped her eyes.

"Human Child," said the Lion. "Where is the Boy?"

"He fell over the cliff," said Jill, and added, "Sir." She didn't know what else to call him, and it sounded cheek to call him nothing.

"How did he come to do that, Human Child?"

"He was trying to stop me from falling, Sir."

"Why were you so near the edge, Human Child?"

"I was showing off, Sir."

"That is a very good answer, Human Child. Do so no more. And now" (here for the first time the Lion's face became a little less stern) "the Boy is safe. I have blown him to Narnia. But your task will be the harder because of what you have done."

"Please, what task, Sir?" said Jill.

"The task for which I called you and him here out of your own world."

This puzzled Jill very much. "It's mistaking me for someone else," she thought. She didn't dare to tell the Lion this, though she felt things would get into a dreadful muddle unless she did.

"Speak your thought, Human Child," said the Lion.

"I was wondering—I mean—could there be some mistake? Because nobody called me and Scrubb, you know. It was we who asked to come here. Scrubb said we were to call to—to Somebody—it was a name I wouldn't know—and perhaps the Somebody would let us in. And we did, and then we found the door open."

"You would not have called to me unless I had been

calling to you," said the Lion.

"Then you are Somebody, Sir?" said Jill.

"I am. And now hear your task. Far from here in the land of Narnia there lives an aged king who is sad because he has no prince of his blood to be king after him. He has no heir because his only son was stolen from him many years ago, and no one in Narnia knows where that prince went or whether he is still alive. But he is. I lay on you this command, that you seek this lost prince until either you have found him and brought him to his father's house, or else died in the attempt, or else gone back to your own world."

"How, please?" said Jill.

"I will tell you, Child," said the Lion. "These are the signs by which I will guide you in your quest. First; as soon as the Boy Eustace sets foot in Narnia, he will meet an old and dear friend. He must greet that friend at once; if he does, you will both have good help. Second; you must journey out of Narnia to the north till you come to the ruined city of the ancient giants. Third; you shall find a writing on a stone in that ruined city, and you must do what the writing tells you. Fourth; you will know the lost prince (if you find him) by this, that he will be the first person you have met in your travels who will ask you to do something in my name, in the name of Aslan."

As the Lion seemed to have finished, Jill thought she should say something. So she said, "Thank you very much. I see."

"Child," said Aslan, in a gentler voice than he had yet used, "perhaps you do not see quite as well as you think. But the first step is to remember. Repeat to me, in order, the four signs."

Jill tried, and didn't get them quite right. So the Lion corrected her, and made her repeat them again and again till she could say them perfectly. He was very patient over this, so that, when it was done, Jill plucked up courage to ask:

"Please, how am I to get to Narnia?"

"On my breath," said the Lion. "I will blow you into the west of the world as I blew Eustace."

"Shall I catch him in time to tell him the first sign? But I suppose it won't matter. If he sees an old friend, he's sure to go and speak to him, isn't he?"

"You will have no time to spare," said the Lion. "That is

why I must send you at once. Come. Walk before me to the edge of the cliff."

Jill remembered very well that if there was no time to spare, that was her own fault. "If I hadn't made such a fool of myself, Scrubb and I would have been going together. And he'd have heard all the instructions as well as me," she thought. So she did as she was told. It was very alarming walking back to the edge of the cliff, especially as the Lion did not walk with her but behind her—making no noise on his soft paws.

But long before she had got anywhere near the edge, the voice behind her said, "Stand still. In a moment I will blow. But, first, remember, remember, remember the signs. Say them to yourself when you wake in the morning and when you lie down at night, and when you wake in the middle of the night. And whatever strange things may happen to you, let nothing turn your mind from following the signs. And secondly, I give you a warning. Here on the mountain I have spoken to you clearly: I will not often do so down in Narnia. Here on the mountain, the air is clear and your mind is clear; as you drop down into Narnia, the air will thicken. Take great care that it does not confuse your mind. And the signs which you have learned here will not look at all as you expect them to look, when you meet them there. That is why it is so important to know them by heart and pay no attention to appearances. Remember the signs and believe the signs. Nothing else matters. And now, daughter of Eve, farewell—"

The voice had been growing softer toward the end of this speech and now it faded away altogether. Jill looked behind her. To her astonishment she saw the cliff already more than a hundred yards behind her, and the Lion himself a speck of bright gold on the edge of it. She had been setting her teeth and clenching her fists for a terrible blast of lion's breath; but the breath had really been so gentle that she had not even noticed the moment at which she left the earth. And now, there was nothing but air for thousands upon thousands of feet below her.

She felt frightened only for a second. For one thing, the world beneath her was so very far away that it seemed to have nothing to do with her. For another, floating on the breath of the Lion was so extremely comfortable. She found she could lie on her back or on her face and twist any way she pleased, just as you can in water (if you've learned to float really well). And because she was moving at the same pace as the breath, there was no wind, and the air seemed beautifully warm. It was not in the least like being in an airplane, because there was no noise and no vibration. If Jill had ever been in a balloon she might have thought it more like that; only better.

When she looked back now she could take in for the first time the real size of the mountain she was leaving. She wondered why a mountain so huge as that was not covered with snow and ice—"but I suppose all that sort of thing is different in this world," thought Jill. Then she looked below her; but she was so high that she couldn't make out whether she was floating over land or sea, nor what speed she was going at.

"By Jove! The signs!" said Jill suddenly. "I'd better repeat them." She was in a panic for a second or two, but she found she could still say them all correctly. "So that's all right," she said, and lay back on the air as if it was a sofa, with a sigh of contentment.

"Well, I do declare," said Jill to herself some hours later, "I've been asleep. Fancy sleeping on air. I wonder if anyone's done it before. I don't suppose they have. Oh bother— Scrubb probably has! On this same journey, a little bit before me. Let's see what it looks like down below."

What it looked like was an enormous, very dark blue plain. There were no hills to be seen, but there were biggish white things moving slowly across it. "Those must be clouds," she thought. "But far bigger than the ones we saw from the cliff. I suppose they're bigger because they're nearer. I must be getting lower. Bother this sun."

The sun which had been high overhead when she began her journey was now getting into her eyes. This meant that it was getting lower, ahead of her. Scrubb was quite right in saying that Jill (I don't know about girls in general) didn't think much about points of the compass. Otherwise she would have known, when the sun began getting in her eyes, that she was traveling pretty nearly due west.

Staring at the blue plain below her, she presently noticed that there were little dots of brighter, paler color in it here and there. "It's the sea!" thought Jill. "I do believe

those are islands." And so they were. She might have felt
rather jealous if she had known that some of them were
islands which Scrubb had seen from a ship's deck and even
landed on; but she didn't know this. Then, later on, she
began to see that there were little wrinkles on the blue flat-
ness: little wrinkles which must be quite big ocean waves if
you were down among them. And now, all along the horizon there was a thick dark line which grew thicker and
darker so quickly that you could see it growing. That was
the first sign she had had of the great speed at which she
was traveling. And she knew that the thickening line must
be land.

Suddenly from her left (for the wind was in the south)
a great white cloud came rushing toward her, this time on
the same level as herself. And before she knew where she
was, she had shot right into the middle of its cold, wet fog-
giness. That took her breath away, but she was in it only for
a moment. She came out blinking in the sunlight and
found her clothes wet. (She had on a blazer and sweater
and shorts and stockings and pretty thick shoes; it had
been a muddy sort of day in England.) She came out lower

than she had gone in; and as soon as she did so she noticed something which, I suppose, she ought to have been expecting, but which came as a surprise and a shock. It was Noises. Up till then she had traveled in total silence. Now, for the first time, she heard the noise of waves and the crying of seagulls. And now, too, she smelled the smell of the sea. There was no mistake about her speed now. She saw two waves meet with a smack and a spout of foam go up between them; but she had hardly seen it before it was a hundred yards behind her. The land was getting nearer at a great pace. She could see mountains far inland, and other nearer mountains on her left. She could see bays and head-lands, woods and fields, stretches of sandy beach. The sound of waves breaking on the shore was growing louder every second and drowning the other sea noises.

Suddenly the land opened right ahead of her. She was coming to the mouth of a river. She was very low now, only a few feet above the water. A wave-top came against her toe and a great splash of foam spurted up, drenching her nearly to the waist. Now she was losing speed. Instead of being carried up the river she was gliding in to the river bank on her left. There were so many things to notice that she could hardly take them all in; a smooth, green lawn, a ship so brightly colored that it looked like an enormous piece of jewelry, towers and battlements, banners fluttering in the air, a crowd, gay clothes, armor, gold, swords, a sound of music. But this was all jumbled. The first thing that she knew clearly was that she had alighted and was standing under a thicket of trees close by the river side, and there, only a few feet away from her, was Scrubb.

The first thing she thought was how very grubby and untidy and generally unimpressive he looked. And the second was "How wet I am!"

Chapter Three

The Sailing of the King

WHAT MADE SCRUBB LOOK SO DINGY (AND JILL TOO, if she could only have seen herself) was the splendor of their surroundings. I had better describe them at once.

Through a cleft in those mountains which Jill had seen far inland as she approached the land, the sunset light was pouring over a level lawn. On the far side of the lawn, its weather-vanes glittering in the light, rose a many-towered and many-turreted castle; the most beautiful castle Jill had ever seen. On the near side was a quay of white marble and, moored to this, the ship: a tall ship with high forecastle and high poop, gilded and crimson, with a great flag at the mast-head, and many banners waving from the decks, and a row of shields, bright as silver, along the bulwarks. The gang-plank was laid to her, and at the foot of it, just ready to go on board, stood an old, old man. He wore a rich mantle of scarlet which opened in front to show his silver mail-shirt. There was a thin circlet of gold on his head. His beard, white as wool, fell nearly to his waist. He stood straight enough, leaning one hand on the shoulder of a richly dressed lord who seemed younger than himself: but you could see he was very old and frail. He looked as if a puff of wind could blow him away, and his eyes were watery.

Immediately in front of the King—who had turned round to speak to his people before going on board the ship—there was a little chair on wheels, and, harnessed to it, a little donkey: not much bigger than a big retriever. In this chair sat a fat little dwarf. He was as richly dressed as the King, but because of his fatness and because he was sitting hunched up among cushions, the effect was quite different: it made him look like a shapeless little bundle of fur and silk and velvet. He was as old as the King, but more hale and hearty, with very keen eyes. His bare head, which was bald and extremely large, shone like a gigantic billiard ball in the sunset light.

Farther back, in a half-circle, stood what Jill at once knew to be courtiers. They were well worth looking at for their clothes and armor alone. As far as that went, they looked more like a flower-bed than a crowd. But what really made Jill open her eyes and mouth as wide as they would go, was the people themselves. If "people" was the right word. For only about one in every five was human. The rest were things you never see in our world. Fauns, satyrs, centaurs: Jill could give a name to these, for she had seen pictures of them. Dwarfs too. And there were a lot of animals she knew as well; bears, badgers, moles, leopards, mice, and various birds. But then they were so very different from the animals which one called by the same names in England. Some of them were much bigger—the mice, for instance, stood on their hind legs and were over two feet high. But quite apart from that, they all looked different. You could see by the expression in their faces that they could talk and think just as well as you could.

"Golly!" thought Jill. "So it's true after all." But next moment she added, "I wonder are they friendly?" For she had just noticed, on the outskirts of the crowd, one or two giants and some people whom she couldn't give a name to at all.

At that moment Aslan and the signs rushed back into her mind. She had forgotten all about them for the last half-hour.

"Scrubb!" she whispered, grabbing his arm. "Scrubb, quick! Do you see anyone you know?"

"So *you've* turned up again, have you?" said Scrubb disagreeably (for which he had some reason). "Well, keep quiet, can't you? I want to listen."

"Don't be a fool," said Jill. "There isn't a moment to lose. Don't you see some old friend here? Because you've got to go and speak to him at once."

"What are you talking about?" said Scrubb.

"It's Aslan—the Lion—says you've got to," said Jill despairingly. "I've seen him."

"Oh, you have, have you? What did he say?"

"He said the very first person you saw in Narnia would be an old friend, and you'd got to speak to him at once."

"Well, there's nobody here I've ever seen in my life before; and anyway, I don't know whether this is Narnia."

"Thought you said you'd been here before," said Jill.

"Well, you thought wrong then."

"Well, I like that! You told me—"

"For heaven's sake dry up and let's hear what they're saying."

The King was speaking to the Dwarf, but Jill couldn't hear what he said. And, as far as she could make out, the Dwarf made no answer, though he nodded and wagged his head a great deal. Then the King raised his voice and addressed the whole court: but his voice was so old and cracked that she could understand very little of his speech—especially since it was all about people and places she had never heard of. When the speech was over, the King stooped down and kissed the Dwarf on both cheeks, straightened himself, raised his right hand as if in blessing, and went, slowly and with feeble steps, up the gangway and on board the ship. The courtiers appeared to be greatly moved by his departure. Handkerchiefs were got out, sounds of sobbing were heard in every direction. The gangway was cast off, trumpets sounded from the poop, and the ship moved away from the quay. (It was being towed by a rowing-boat, but Jill didn't see that.)

"Now—" said Scrubb, but he didn't get any further because at that moment a large white object—Jill thought for a second that it was a kite—came gliding through the air and alighted at his feet. It was a white owl, but so big that it stood as high as a good-sized dwarf.

It blinked and peered as if it were short-sighted, and put its head a little to one side, and said in a soft, hooting kind of voice:

"Tu-whoo, tu-whoo! Who are you two?"

"My name's Scrubb, and this is Pole," said Eustace. "Would you mind telling us where we are?"

"In the land of Narnia, at the King's castle of Cair Paravel."

"Is that the King who's just taken ship?"

"Too true, too true," said the Owl sadly, shaking its big head. "But who are you? There's something magic about you two. I saw you arrive: you *flew*. Everyone else was so busy seeing the King off that nobody knew. Except me. I happened to notice you, you flew."

"We were sent here by Aslan," said Eustace in a low voice.

"Tu-whoo, tu-whoo!" said the Owl, ruffling out its feathers. "This is almost too much for me, so early in the evening. I'm not quite myself till the sun's down."

"And we've been sent to find the lost Prince," said Jill, who had been anxiously waiting to get into the conversation.

"It's the first I've heard about it," said Eustace. "What prince?"

"You had better come and speak to the Lord Regent at once," it said. "That's him, over there in the donkey carriage—Trumpkin the Dwarf." The bird turned and began leading the way, muttering to itself, "Whoo! Tu-whoo! What a to-do! I can't think clearly yet. It's too early."

"What is the King's name?" asked Eustace.

"Caspian the Tenth," said the Owl. And Jill wondered why Scrubb had suddenly pulled up short in his walk and turned an extraordinary color. She thought she had never seen him look so sick about anything. But before she had time to ask any questions they had reached the dwarf, who was just gathering up the reins of his donkey and preparing to drive back to the castle. The crowd of courtiers had broken up and were going in the same direction, by ones and twos and little knots, like people coming away from watching a game or a race.

"Tu-whoo! Ahem! Lord Regent," said the Owl, stooping down a little and holding its beak near the Dwarf's ear.

"Heh? What's that?" said the Dwarf.

"Two strangers, my lord," said the Owl.

"Rangers! What d'ye mean?" said the Dwarf. "I see two uncommonly grubby man-cubs. What do they want?"

"My name's Jill," said Jill, pressing forward. She was very eager to explain the important business on which they had come.

"The girl's called Jill," said the Owl, as loud as it could.

"What's that?" said the Dwarf. "The girls are all killed! I don't believe a word of it. What girls? Who killed 'em?"

"Only one girl, my lord," said the Owl. "Her name is Jill."

"Speak up, speak up," said the Dwarf. "Don't stand there buzzing and twittering in my ear. Who's been killed?"

"Nobody's been killed," hooted the Owl.

"Who?"

"NOBODY."

"All right, all right. You needn't shout. I'm not so deaf as all that. What do you mean by coming here to tell me that nobody's been killed? Why should anyone have been killed?"

"Better tell him I'm Eustace," said Scrubb.

"The boy's Eustace, my lord," hooted the Owl as loud as it could.

"Useless?" said the Dwarf irritably. "I dare say he is. Is that any reason for bringing him to court? Hey?"

"Not useless," said the Owl. "EUSTACE."

"Used to it, is he? I don't know what you're talking about, I'm sure. I tell you what it is, Master Glimfeather; when I was a young Dwarf there used to be *talking* beasts and birds in this country who really could talk. There wasn't all this mumbling and muttering and whispering. It wouldn't have been tolerated for a moment. Not for a moment, Sir. Urnus, my trumpet please—"

A little Faun who had been standing quietly beside the Dwarf's elbow all this time now handed him a silver ear-trumpet. It was made like the musical instrument called a serpent, so that the tube curled right round the Dwarf's neck. While he was getting it settled the Owl, Glimfeather, suddenly said to the children in a whisper:

"My brain's a bit clearer now. Don't say anything about the lost Prince. I'll explain later. It wouldn't do, wouldn't do, Tu-Whoo! Oh, *what* a to-do!"

"Now," said the Dwarf, "if you *have* anything sensible to say, Master Glimfeather, try and say it. Take a deep breath and don't attempt to speak too quickly."

With help from the children, and in spite of a fit of coughing on the part of the Dwarf, Glimfeather explained that the strangers had been sent by Aslan to visit the court of Narnia. The Dwarf glanced quickly up at them with a new expression in his eyes.

"Sent by the Lion Himself, hey?" he said. "And from— m'm—from that other Place—beyond the world's end, hey?"

"Yes, my lord," bawled Eustace into the trumpet.

"Son of Adam and Daughter of Eve, hey?" said the Dwarf. But people at Experiment House haven't heard of Adam and Eve, so Jill and Eustace couldn't answer this. But the Dwarf didn't seem to notice.

"Well, my dears," he said, taking first one and then the other by the hand and bowing his head a little. "You are very heartily welcome. If the good King, my poor Master, had not this very hour set sail for Seven Isles, he would have been glad of your coming. It would have brought back his youth to him for a moment—for a moment. And now, it is high time for supper. You shall tell me your business in full council tomorrow morning. Master Glimfeather, see that bedchambers and suitable clothes and all else are provided for these guests in the most honorable fashion. And— Glimfeather—in your ear—"

Here the Dwarf put his mouth close to the Owl's head and, no doubt, intended to whisper: but, like other deaf people, he wasn't a very good judge of his own voice, and both children heard him say, "See that they're properly washed."

After that, the Dwarf touched up his donkey and it set off toward the castle at something between a trot and a waddle (it was a very fat little beast), while the Faun, the Owl, and the children followed at a rather slower pace. The sun had set and the air was growing cool.

They went across the lawn and then through an orchard and so to the North Gate of Cair Paravel, which stood wide open. Inside, they found a grassy courtyard. Lights were already showing from the windows of the great hall on their right and from a more complicated mass of buildings straight ahead. Into these the Owl led them, and there a most delightful person was called to look after Jill. She was not much taller than Jill herself, and a good deal slenderer, but obviously full grown, graceful as a willow, and her hair was willowy too, and there seemed to be moss in it. She brought Jill to a round room in one of the turrets, where there was a little bath sunk in the floor and a fire of sweet-smelling woods burning on the flat hearth and a lamp hanging by a silver chain from the vaulted roof. The window looked west into the strange land of Narnia, and Jill saw the red remains of the sunset still glowing behind distant mountains. It made her long for more adventures and feel sure that this was only the beginning.

When she had had her bath, and brushed her hair, and put on the clothes that had been laid out for her—they were the kind that not only felt nice, but looked nice and smelled nice and made nice sounds when you moved as well—she would have gone back to gaze out of that exciting window, but she was interrupted by a bang on the door.

"Come in," said Jill. And in came Scrubb, also bathed and splendidly dressed in Narnian clothes. But his face didn't look as if he were enjoying it.

"Oh, here you are at last," he said crossly, flinging himself into a chair. "I've been trying to find you for ever so long."

"Well, now you have," said Jill. "I say, Scrubb, isn't it all simply too exciting and scrumptious for words." She had forgotten all about the signs and the lost Prince for the moment.

"Oh! That's what you think, is it?" said Scrubb: and then, after a pause, "I wish to goodness we'd never come."

"Why on earth?"

"I can't bear it," said Scrubb. "Seeing the King—Caspian—a doddering old man like that. It's—it's frightful."

"Why, what harm does it do you?"

"Oh, you don't understand. Now that I come to think of it, you couldn't. I didn't tell you that this world has a different time from ours."

"How do you mean?"

"The time you spend here doesn't take up any of our time. Do you see? I mean, however long we spend here, we shall still get back to Experiment House at the moment we left it—"

"That won't be much fun—"

"Oh, dry up! Don't keep interrupting. And when you're back in England—in our world—you can't tell how time is going here. It might be any number of years in Narnia while we're having one year at home. The Pevensies explained it all to me, but, like a fool, I forgot about it. And now apparently it's been about seventy years—Narnian years—since I was here last. Do you see now? And I come back and find Caspian an old, old man."

"Then the King *was* an old friend of yours!" said Jill. A horrid thought had struck her.

"I should jolly well think he was," said Scrubb miserably. "About as good a friend as a chap could have. And last time he was only a few years older than me. And to see that old man with a white beard, and to remember Caspian as he was the morning we captured the Lone Islands, or in the fight with the Sea Serpent—oh, it's frightful. It's worse than coming back and finding him dead."

"Oh, shut up," said Jill impatiently. "It's far worse than you think. We've muffed the first Sign." Of course Scrubb did not understand this. Then Jill told him about her conversation with Aslan and the four signs and the task of finding the lost prince which had been laid upon them.

"So you see," she wound up, "you did see an old friend, just as Aslan said, and you ought to have gone and spoken to him at once. And now you haven't, and everything is going wrong from the very beginning."

"But how was I to know?" said Scrubb.

"If you'd only listened to me when I tried to tell you, we'd be all right," said Jill.

"Yes, and if you hadn't played the fool on the edge of that cliff and jolly nearly murdered me—all right, I said *murder*, and I'll say it again as often as I like, so keep your hair on—we'd have come together and both known what to do."

"I suppose he *was* the very first person you saw?" said Jill. "You must have been here hours before me. Are you sure you didn't see anyone else first?"

"I was only here about a minute before you," said Scrubb. "He must have blown you quicker than me. Making up for lost time: the time *you* lost."

"Don't be a perfect beast, Scrubb," said Jill. "Hallo! What's that?"

It was the castle bell ringing for supper, and thus what looked like turning into a first-rate quarrel was happily cut short. Both had a good appetite by this time.

Supper in the great hall of the castle was the most splendid thing either of them had ever seen; for though Eustace had been in that world before, he had spent his

whole visit at sea and knew nothing of the glory and courtesy of the Narnians at home in their own land. The banners hung from the roof, and each course came in with
trumpeters and kettledrums. There were soups that would
make your mouth water to think of, and the lovely fishes
called pavenders, and venison and peacock and pies, and
ices and jellies and fruit and nuts, and all manner of wines
and fruit drinks. Even Eustace cheered up and admitted
that it was "something like." And when all the serious
eating and drinking was over, a blind poet came forward
and struck up the grand old tale of Prince Cor and Aravis
and the horse Bree, which is called *The Horse and His Boy*
and tells of an adventure that happened in Narnia and
Calormen and the lands between, in the Golden Age
when Peter was High King in Cair Paravel. (I haven't time
to tell it now, though it is well worth hearing.)

When they were dragging themselves upstairs to bed,
yawning their heads off, Jill said, "I bet we sleep well
tonight," for it had been a full day. Which just shows
how little anyone knows what is going to happen to
them next.

Chapter Four

A Parliament of Owls

IT IS A VERY FUNNY THING THAT THE SLEEPIER YOU are, the longer you take about getting to bed; especially if you are lucky enough to have a fire in your room. Jill felt she couldn't even start undressing unless she sat down in front of the fire for a bit first. And once she had sat down, she didn't want to get up again. She had already said to herself about five times, "I must go to bed," when she was startled by a tap on the window.

She got up, pulled the curtain, and at first saw nothing

but darkness. Then she jumped and started backward, for something very large had dashed itself against the window, giving a sharp tap on the glass as it did so. A very unpleasant idea came into her head—"Suppose they have giant moths in this country! Ugh!" But then the thing came back, and this time she was almost sure she saw a beak, and that the beak had made the tapping noise. "It's some huge bird," thought Jill. "Could it be an eagle?" She didn't very much want a visit even from an eagle, but she opened the window and looked out. Instantly, with a great whirring noise, the creature alighted on the window-sill and stood there filling up the whole window, so that Jill had to step back to make room for it. It was the Owl.

"Hush, hush! Tu-whoo, tu-whoo," said the Owl. "Don't make a noise. Now, are you two really in earnest about what you've got to do?"

"About the lost Prince, you mean?" said Jill. "Yes, we've got to be." For now she remembered the Lion's voice and face, which she had nearly forgotten during the feasting and story-telling in the hall.

"Good!" said the Owl. "Then there's no time to waste.

You must get away from here at once. I'll go and wake the other human. Then I'll come back for you. You'd better change those court clothes and put on something you can travel in. I'll be back in two twos. Tu-whoo!" And without waiting for an answer, he was gone.

If Jill had been more used to adventures, she might have doubted the Owl's word, but this never occurred to her: and in the exciting idea of a midnight escape she forgot her sleepiness. She changed back into sweater and shorts—there was a guide's knife on the belt of the shorts which might come in useful—and added a few of the things that had been left in the room for her by the girl with the willowy hair. She chose a short cloak that came down to her knees and had a hood ("just the thing, if it rains," she thought), a few handkerchiefs and a comb. Then she sat down and waited.

She was getting sleepy again when the Owl returned.

"Now we're ready," it said.

"You'd better lead the way," said Jill. "I don't know all these passages yet."

"Tu-whoo!" said the Owl. "We're not going through

the castle. That would never do. You must ride on me. We shall fly."

"Oh!" said Jill, and stood with her mouth open, not much liking the idea. "Shan't I be far too heavy for you?"

"Tu-whoo, tu-whoo! Don't you be a fool. I've already carried the other one. Now. But we'll put out that lamp first."

As soon as the lamp was out, the bit of night which you saw through the window looked less dark—no longer black, but gray. The Owl stood on the window-sill with his back to the room and raised his wings. Jill had to climb onto his short fat body and get her knees under the wings and grip tight. The feathers felt beautifully warm and soft but there was nothing to hold on by. "I wonder how Scrubb liked *his* ride!" thought Jill. And just as she was thinking this, with a horrid plunge they had left the window-sill, and the wings were making a flurry round her ears, and the night air, rather cool and damp, was flying in her face.

It was much lighter than she expected, and though the sky was overcast, one patch of watery silver showed where the moon was hiding above the clouds. The fields beneath her looked gray, and the trees black. There was a certain amount of wind—a hushing, ruffling sort of wind which meant that rain was coming soon.

The Owl wheeled round so that the castle was now ahead of them. Very few of the windows showed lights. They flew right over it, northward, crossing the river: the air grew colder, and Jill thought she could see the white reflection of the Owl in the water beneath her. But soon they were on the north bank of the river, flying above wooded country.

The Owl snapped at something which Jill couldn't see.

"Oh, don't, please!" said Jill. "Don't jerk like that. You nearly threw me off."

"I beg your pardon," said the Owl. "I was just nabbing a bat. There's nothing so sustaining, in a small way, as a nice plump little bat. Shall I catch you one?"

"No, thanks," said Jill with a shudder.

He was flying a little lower now and a large, black-looking object was looming up toward them. Jill had just time to see that it was a tower—a partly ruinous tower, with a lot of ivy on it, she thought—when she found herself ducking to avoid the archway of a window, as the Owl squeezed with her through the ivied cobwebby opening, out of the fresh, gray night into a dark place inside the top of the tower. It was rather fusty inside and, the moment she slipped off the Owl's back, she knew (as one usually does somehow) that it was quite crowded. And when voices began saying out of the darkness from every direction "Tu-whoo! Tu-whoo!" she knew it was crowded with owls. She was rather relieved when a very different voice said:

"Is that you, Pole?"

"Is that you, Scrubb?" said Jill.

"Now," said Glimfeather, "I think we're all here. Let us hold a parliament of owls."

"Tu-whoo, tu-whoo. True for you. That's the right thing to do," said several voices.

"Half a moment," said Scrubb's voice. "There's something I want to say first."

"Do, do, do," said the owls; and Jill said, "Fire ahead."

"I suppose all you chaps—owls, I mean," said Scrubb, "I suppose you all know that King Caspian the Tenth, in his

young days, sailed to the eastern end of the world. Well, I
was with him on that journey: with him and Reepicheep
the Mouse, and the Lord Drinian and all of them. I know
it sounds hard to believe, but people don't grow older in
our world at the same speed as they do in yours. And what
I want to say is this, that I'm the King's man; and if this parliament of owls is any sort of plot against the King, I'm
having nothing to do with it."

"Tu-whoo, tu-whoo, we're all the King's owls too," said
the owls.

"What's it all about then?" said Scrubb.

"It's only this," said Glimfeather. "That if the Lord
Regent, the Dwarf Trumpkin, hears you are going to look
for the lost Prince, he won't let you start. He'd keep you
under lock and key sooner."

"Great Scott!" said Scrubb. "You don't mean that
Trumpkin is a traitor? I used to hear a lot about him in the
old days, at sea. Caspian—the King, I mean—trusted him
absolutely."

"Oh no," said a voice. "Trumpkin's no traitor. But more
than thirty champions (knights, centaurs, good giants,
and all sorts) have at one time or another set out to look for

the lost Prince, and none of them have ever come back. And at last the King said he was not going to have all the bravest Narnians destroyed in the search for his son. And now nobody is allowed to go."

"But surely he'd let *us* go," said Scrubb. "When he knew who I was and who had sent me."

("Sent both of us," put in Jill.)

"Yes," said Glimfeather, "I think, very likely, he would. But the King's away. And Trumpkin will stick to the rules. He's as true as steel, but he's deaf as a post and very peppery. You could never make him see that this might be the time for making an exception to the rule."

"You might think he'd take some notice of *us*, because we're owls and everyone knows how wise owls are," said someone else. "But he's so old now he'd only say, 'You're a mere chick. I remember you when you were an egg. Don't come trying to teach *me*, Sir. Crabs and crumpets!'"

This owl imitated Trumpkin's voice rather well, and there were sounds of owlish laughter all round. The children began to see that the Narnians all felt about Trumpkin as people feel at school about some crusty teacher, whom everyone is a little afraid of and everyone makes fun of and nobody really dislikes.

"How long is the King going to be away?" asked Scrubb.

"If only we knew!" said Glimfeather. "You see, there has been a rumor lately that Aslan himself has been seen in the islands—in Terebinthia, I think it was. And the King said he would make one more attempt before he died to see Aslan face to face again, and ask his advice about who is to be King after him. But we're all afraid that, if he doesn't meet Aslan in Terebinthia, he'll go on east, to Seven Isles and the Lone Islands—and on and on. He never talks about it, but we all know he has never forgotten that voyage to the world's end. I'm sure in his heart of hearts he wants to go there again."

"Then there's no good waiting for him to come back?" said Jill.

"No, no good," said the Owl. "Oh, what a to-do! If only you two had known and spoken to him at once! He'd have arranged everything—probably given you an army to go with you in search of the Prince."

Jill kept quiet at this and hoped Scrubb would be sporting enough not to tell all the owls why this hadn't happened. He was, or very nearly. That is, he only muttered under his breath, "Well, it wasn't *my* fault," before saying out loud:

"Very well. We'll have to manage without it. But there's just one thing more I want to know. If this owls' parliament, as you call it, is all fair and above board and means no mischief, why does it have to be so jolly secret—meeting in a ruin at the dead of night, and all that?"

"Tu-whoo! Tu-whoo!" hooted several owls. "Where should we meet? When would anyone meet except at night?"

"You see," explained Glimfeather, "most of the creatures in Narnia have such unnatural habits. They do things by day, in broad blazing sunlight (ugh!) when everyone ought to be asleep. And, as a result, at night they're so blind and stupid that you can't get a word out of them. So we owls have got into the habit of meeting at sensible hours, on our own, when we want to talk about things."

"I see," said Scrubb. "Well now, let's get on. Tell us all about the lost Prince." Then an old owl, not Glimfeather, related the story.

About ten years ago, it appeared, when Rilian, the son of Caspian, was a very young knight, he rode with the Queen his mother on a May morning in the north parts of Narnia. They had many squires and ladies with them and all wore garlands of fresh leaves on their heads and horns at their sides; but they had no hounds with them, for they were maying, not hunting. In the warm part of the day they came to a pleasant glade where a fountain flowed freshly out of the earth, and there they dismounted and ate and drank and were merry. After a time the Queen felt sleepy, and they spread cloaks for her on the grassy bank, and Prince Rilian with the rest of the party went a little way from her, that their tales and laughter might not wake her. And so, presently, a great serpent came out of the thick wood and stung the Queen in her hand. All heard her cry out and rushed toward her, and Rilian was first at her side. He saw the worm gliding away from her and made after it with his sword drawn. It was great, shining, and as green as poison, so that he could see it well: but it glided away into thick bushes and he could not come at it. So he returned to his mother, and found them all busy about her. But they were busy in vain, for at the first glance of her face Rilian knew that no physic in the world would do her good. As long as the life was in her she seemed to be trying hard to tell him something. But she could not speak clearly and, whatever her message was, she died without delivering it. It was then hardly ten minutes since they had first heard her cry.

They carried the dead Queen back to Cair Paravel, and she was bitterly mourned by Rilian and by the King, and by all Narnia. She had been a great lady, wise and gracious and happy, King Caspian's bride whom he had brought home from the eastern end of the world. And men said that the blood of the stars flowed in her veins. The Prince took his mother's death very hardly, as well he might. After that, he was always riding on the northern marches of Narnia, hunting for that venomous worm, to kill it and be avenged. No one remarked much on this, though the Prince came home from these wanderings looking tired and distraught. But about a month after the Queen's death, some said they could see a change in him. There was a look in his eyes as of a man who has seen visions, and though he would be out all day, his horse did not bear the signs of hard riding. His chief friend among the older courtiers was the Lord Drinian, he who had been his father's captain on that great voyage to the east parts of the world.

One evening Drinian said to the Prince, "Your Highness must soon give over seeking the worm. There is no true vengeance on a witless brute as there might be on a man. You weary yourself in vain." The Prince answered him, "My Lord, I have almost forgotten the worm this seven days." Drinian asked him why, if that were so, he rode so continually in the northern woods. "My lord," said the Prince, "I have seen there the most beautiful thing that was ever made." "Fair Prince," said Drinian, "of your courtesy let me ride with you tomorrow, that I also may see this fair thing." "With a good will," said Rilian.

Then in good time on the next day they saddled their horses and rode a great gallop into the northern woods and alighted at the same fountain where the Queen got her death. Drinian thought it strange that the Prince should choose that place of all places, to linger in. And there they rested till it came to high noon: and at noon Drinian looked up and saw the most beautiful lady he had ever seen; and she stood at the north side of the fountain and said no word but beckoned to the Prince with her hand as if she bade him come to her. And she was tall and great, shining, and wrapped in a thin garment as green as poison. And the Prince stared at her like a man out of his wits. But suddenly the lady was gone, Drinian knew not where; and they two returned to Cair Paravel. It stuck in Drinian's mind that this shining green woman was evil.

Drinian doubted very much whether he ought not to tell this adventure to the King, but he had little wish to be a blab and a tale-bearer and so he held his tongue. But afterward he wished he had spoken. For next day Prince Rilian rode out alone. That night he came not back, and from that hour no trace of him was ever found in Narnia nor any neighboring land, and neither his horse nor his hat nor his cloak nor anything else was ever found. Then Drinian in the bitterness of his heart went to Caspian and said, "Lord King, slay me speedily as a great traitor: for by my silence I have destroyed your son." And he told him the story. Then Caspian caught up a battle-axe and rushed upon the Lord Drinian to kill him, and Drinian stood still as a stock for the death blow. But when the axe was raised, Caspian suddenly threw it away and cried out, "I have lost my queen and my son: shall I lose my friend also?" And he fell upon the Lord Drinian's neck and embraced him and both wept, and their friendship was not broken.

Such was the story of Rilian. And when it was over, Jill said, "I bet that serpent and that woman were the same person."

"True, true, we think the same as you," hooted the owls.

"But we don't think she killed the Prince," said Glimfeather, "because no bones—"

"We know she didn't," said Scrubb. "Aslan told Pole he was still alive somewhere."

"That almost makes it worse," said the oldest owl. "It means she has some use for him, and some deep scheme against Narnia. Long, long ago, at the very beginning, a White Witch came out of the North and bound our land in snow and ice for a hundred years. And we think this may be some of the same crew."

"Very well, then," said Scrubb. "Pole and I have got to find this Prince. Can you help us?"

"Have you any clue, you two?" asked Glimfeather.

"Yes," said Scrubb. "We know we've got to go north. And we know we've got to reach the ruins of a giant city."

At this there was a greater tu-whooing than ever, and noises of birds shifting their feet and ruffling their feathers, and then all the owls started speaking at once. They all explained how very sorry they were that they themselves could not go with the children on their search for the lost Prince. "You'd want to travel by day, and we'd want to travel by night," they said. "It wouldn't do, wouldn't do." One or two owls added that even here in the ruined tower it wasn't nearly so dark as it had been when they began, and that the parliament had been going on quite long enough. In fact, the mere mention of a journey to the ruined city of giants seemed to have damped the spirits of those birds. But Glimfeather said:

"If they want to go that way—into Ettinsmoor—we must take them to one of the Marsh-wiggles. They're the only people who can help them much."

"True, true. Do," said the owls.

"Come on, then," said Glimfeather. "I'll take one. Who'll take the other? It must be done tonight."

"I will: as far as the Marsh-wiggles," said another owl.

"Are you ready?" said Glimfeather to Jill.

"I think Pole's asleep," said Scrubb.

Chapter Five

Puddleglum

JILL WAS ASLEEP. EVER SINCE THE OWLS' PARLIAMENT began she had been yawning terribly and now she had dropped off. She was not at all pleased at being waked again, and at finding herself lying on bare boards in a dusty belfry sort of place, completely dark, and almost completely full of owls. She was even less pleased when she heard that they had to set off for somewhere else—and not, apparently, for bed—on the Owl's back.

"Oh, come on, Pole, buck up," said Scrubb's voice.

"After all, it *is* an adventure."

"I'm sick of adventures," said Jill crossly.

She did, however, consent to climb on to Glimfeather's back and was thoroughly waked up (for a while) by the unexpected coldness of the air when he flew out with her into the night. The moon had disappeared and there were no stars. Far behind her she could see a single lighted window well above the ground; doubtless, in one of the towers of Cair Paravel. It made her long to be back in that delightful bedroom, snug in bed, watching the firelight on the walls. She put her hands under her cloak and wrapped it tightly round her. It was uncanny to hear two voices in the dark air a little distance away; Scrubb and his owl were talking to one another. "*He* doesn't sound tired," thought Jill. She did not realize that he had been on great adventures in that world before and that the Narnian air was bringing back to him a strength he had won when he sailed the Eastern Seas with King Caspian.

Jill had to pinch herself to keep awake, for she knew that if she dozed on Glimfeather's back she would probably fall off. When at last the two owls ended their flight, she climbed stiffly off Glimfeather and found herself on flat ground. A chilly wind was blowing and they appeared to be in a place without trees. "Tu-whoo, tu-whoo!" Glimfeather was calling. "Wake up, Puddleglum. Wake up. It is on the Lion's business."

For a long time there was no reply. Then, a long way off, a dim light appeared and began to come nearer. With it came a voice.

"Owls ahoy!" it said. "What is it? Is the King dead? Has an enemy landed in Narnia? Is it a flood? Or dragons?"

When the light reached them, it turned out to be that of a large lantern. Jill could see very little of the person who held it. He seemed to be all legs and arms. The owls were talking to him, explaining everything, but she was too tired to listen. She tried to wake herself up a bit when she realized that they were saying goodbye to her. But she could never afterward remember much except that, sooner or later, she and Scrubb were stooping to enter a low doorway and then (oh, thank heavens) were lying down on something soft and warm, and a voice was saying:

"There you are. Best we can do. You'll lie cold and hard.

Damp too, I shouldn't wonder. Won't sleep a wink, most likely; even if there isn't a thunderstorm or a flood or a wigwam doesn't fall down on top of us all, as I've known them to do. Must make the best of it—" But she was fast asleep before the voice had ended.

When the children woke late the next morning they found that they were lying, very dry and warm, on beds of straw in a dark place. A triangular opening let in the daylight.

"Where on earth are we?" asked Jill.

"In the wigwam of a Marsh-wiggle," said Eustace.

"A what?"

"A Marsh-wiggle. Don't ask me what it is. I couldn't see it last night. I'm getting up. Let's go and look for it."

"How beastly one feels after sleeping in one's clothes," said Jill, sitting up.

"I was just thinking how nice it was not to have to dress," said Eustace.

"Or wash either, I suppose," said Jill scornfully. But Scrubb had already got up, yawned, shaken himself, and crawled out of the wigwam. Jill did the same.

What they found outside was quite unlike the bit of Narnia they had seen on the day before. They were on a great flat plain which was cut into countless little islands by countless channels of water. The islands were covered with coarse grass and bordered with reeds and rushes. Sometimes there were beds of rushes about an acre in extent. Clouds of birds were constantly alighting in them and rising from them again—duck, snipe, bitterns, herons. Many wigwams like that in which they had passed the night could be seen dotted about, but all at a good distance from one another; for Marsh-wiggles are people who like privacy. Except for the fringe of the forest several miles to the south and west of them, there was not a tree in sight. Eastward the flat marsh stretched to low sand-hills on the horizon, and you could tell by the salt tang in the wind which blew from that direction that the sea lay over there. To the North there were low pale-colored hills, in places bastioned with rock. The rest was all flat marsh. It would have been a depressing place on a wet evening. Seen under a morning sun, with a fresh wind blowing, and the air filled with the crying of birds, there was something fine and fresh

and clean about its loneliness. The children felt their spirits rise.

"Where has the thingummy got to, I wonder?" said Jill.

"The Marsh-wiggle," said Scrubb, as if he were rather
proud of knowing the word. "I expect—hullo, that must be
him." And then they both saw him, sitting with his back to
them, fishing, about fifty yards away. He had been hard to
see at first because he was nearly the same color as the marsh
and because he sat so still.

"I suppose we'd better go and speak to him," said Jill.
Scrubb nodded. They both felt a little nervous.

As they drew nearer, the figure turned its head and
showed them a long thin face with rather sunken cheeks,
a tightly shut mouth, a sharp nose, and no beard. He was
wearing a high, pointed hat like a steeple, with an enor-
mously wide flat brim. The hair, if it could be called hair,
which hung over his large ears was greeny-gray, and each
lock was flat rather than round, so that they were like tiny
reeds. His expression was solemn, his complexion muddy,
and you could see at once that he took a serious view of life.

"Good morning, Guests," he said. "Though when I say

good I don't mean it won't probably turn to rain or it might be snow, or fog, or thunder. You didn't get any sleep, I dare say."

"Yes we did, though," said Jill. "We had a lovely night."

"Ah," said the Marsh-wiggle, shaking his head. "I see you're making the best of a bad job. That's right. You've been well brought up, you have. You've learned to put a good face on things."

"Please, we don't know your name," said Scrubb.

"Puddleglum's my name. But it doesn't matter if you forget it. I can always tell you again."

The children sat down on each side of him. They now saw that he had very long legs and arms, so that although his body was not much bigger than a dwarf's, he would be taller than most men when he stood up. The fingers of his hands were webbed like a frog's, and so were his bare feet which dangled in the muddy water. He was dressed in earth-colored clothes that hung loose about him.

"I'm trying to catch a few eels to make an eel stew for our dinner," said Puddleglum. "Though I shouldn't wonder if I didn't get any. And you won't like them much if I do."

"Why not?" asked Scrubb.

"Why, it's not in reason that you should like our sort of victuals, though I've no doubt you'll put a bold face on it. All the same, while I am a catching them, if you two could try to light the fire—no harm trying—! The wood's behind the wigwam. It may be wet. You could light it inside the wigwam, and then we'd get all the smoke in our eyes. Or you could light it outside, and then the rain would come and put it out. Here's my tinder-box. You wouldn't know how to use it, I expect."

But Scrubb had learnt that sort of thing on his last adventure. The children ran back together to the wigwam, found the wood (which was perfectly dry) and succeeded in lighting a fire with rather less than the usual difficulty. Then Scrubb sat and took care of it while Jill went and had some sort of wash—not a very nice one—in the nearest channel. After that she saw to the fire and he had a wash. Both felt a good deal fresher, but very hungry.

Presently the Marsh-wiggle joined them. In spite of his expectation of catching no eels, he had a dozen or so, which he had already skinned and cleaned. He put a big pot on, mended the fire, and lit his pipe. Marsh-wiggles smoke a very strange, heavy sort of tobacco (some people say they mix it with mud) and the children noticed the smoke from Puddleglum's pipe hardly rose in the air at all. It trickled out of the bowl and downward and drifted along the ground like a mist. It was very black and set Scrubb coughing.

"Now," said Puddleglum. "Those eels will take a mortal long time to cook, and either of you might faint with hunger before they're done. I knew a little girl—but I'd better not tell you that story. It might lower your spirits, and that's a thing I never do. So, to keep your minds off your hunger, we may as well talk about our plans."

"Yes, do, let's," said Jill. "Can you help us to find Prince Rilian?"

The Marsh-wiggle sucked in his cheeks till they were hollower than you would have thought possible. "Well, I don't know that you'd call it *help*," he said. "I don't know that anyone can exactly *help*. It stands to reason we're not likely to get very far on a journey to the North, not at this time of the year, with the winter coming on soon and all. And an early winter too, by the look of things. But you mustn't let that make you down-hearted. Very likely, what with enemies, and mountains, and rivers to cross, and losing our way, and next to nothing to eat, and sore feet, we'll hardly notice the weather. And if we don't get far enough to do any good, we may get far enough not to get back in a hurry."

Both children noticed that he said "we," not "you," and both exclaimed at the same moment, "Are you coming with us?"

"Oh yes, I'm coming of course. Might as well, you see. I don't suppose we shall ever see the King back in Narnia, now that he's once set off for foreign parts; and he had a nasty cough when he left. Then there's Trumpkin. He's failing fast. And you'll find there'll have been a bad harvest after this terrible dry summer. And I shouldn't wonder if some enemy attacked us. Mark my words."

"And how shall we start?" said Scrubb.

"Well," said the Marsh-wiggle very slowly, "all the others who ever went looking for Prince Rilian started from the same fountain where Lord Drinian saw the lady. They went north, mostly. And as none of them ever came back, we can't exactly say how they got on."

"We've got to start by finding a ruined city of giants," said Jill. "Aslan said so."

"Got to start by *finding* it, have we?" answered Puddleglum. "Not allowed to start by *looking* for it, I suppose?"

"That's what I meant, of course," said Jill. "And then, when we've found it—"

"Yes, when!" said Puddleglum very drily.

"Doesn't anyone know where it is?" asked Scrubb.

"I don't know about Anyone," said Puddleglum. "And I won't say I haven't heard of that Ruined City. You wouldn't start from the fountain, though. You'd have to go across Ettinsmoor. That's where the Ruined City is, if it's anywhere. But I've been as far in that direction as most people and I never got to any ruins, so I won't deceive you."

"Where's Ettinsmoor?" said Scrubb.

"Look over there northward," said Puddleglum, pointing with his pipe. "See those hills and bits of cliff? That's the beginning of Ettinsmoor. But there's a river between it and us; the river Shribble. No bridges, of course."

"I suppose we can ford it, though," said Scrubb.

"Well, it *has* been forded," admitted the Marsh-wiggle.

"Perhaps we shall meet people on Ettinsmoor who can tell us the way," said Jill.

"You're right about meeting people," said Puddleglum.

"What sort of people live there?" she asked.

"It's not for me to say they aren't all right in their own way," answered Puddleglum. "If you like their way."

"Yes, but what *are* they?" pressed Jill. "There are so many queer creatures in this country. I mean, are they animals, or birds, or dwarfs, or what?"

The Marsh-wiggle gave a long whistle. "Phew!" he said. "Don't you know? I thought the owls had told you. They're giants."

Jill winced. She had never liked giants even in books, and she had once met one in a nightmare. Then she saw Scrubb's face, which had turned rather green, and thought to herself, "I bet he's in a worse funk than I am." That made her feel braver.

"The King told me long ago," said Scrubb, "—that time when I was with him at sea—that he'd jolly well beaten those giants in war and made them pay him tribute."

"That's true enough," said Puddleglum. "They're at peace with us all right. As long as we stay on our own side of the Shribble, they won't do us any harm. Over on their side, on the Moor—Still, there's always a chance. If we don't get near any of them, and if none of them forget themselves, and if we're not seen, it's just possible we might get a long way."

"Look here!" said Scrubb, suddenly losing his temper, as people so easily do when they have been frightened. "I don't believe the whole thing can be half as bad as you're making out; any more than the beds in the wigwam were hard or the wood was wet. I don't think Aslan would ever have sent us if there was so little chance as all that."

He quite expected the Marsh-wiggle to give him an angry reply, but he only said, "That's the spirit, Scrubb. That's the way to talk. Put a good face on it. But we all need to be very careful about our tempers, seeing all the hard times we shall have to go through together. Won't do to quarrel, you know. At any rate, don't begin it too soon. I know these expeditions usually *end* that way: knifing one another, I shouldn't wonder, before all's done. But the longer we can keep off it—"

"Well, if you feel it's so hopeless," interrupted Scrubb, "I think you'd better stay behind. Pole and I can go on alone, can't we, Pole?"

"Shut up and don't be an ass, Scrubb," said Jill hastily, terrified lest the Marsh-wiggle should take him at his word.

"Don't you lose heart, Pole," said Puddleglum. "I'm coming, sure and certain. I'm not going to lose an opportunity like this. It will do me good. They all say—I mean, the other wiggles all say—that I'm too flighty; don't take life seriously enough. If they've said it once, they've said it a thousand times. 'Puddleglum,' they've said, 'you're altogether too full of bobance and bounce and high spirits. You've got to learn that life isn't all fricasseed frogs and eel pie. You want something to sober you down a bit. We're only saying it for your own good, Puddleglum.' That's what they say. Now a job like this—a journey up north just as winter's beginning, looking for a Prince that probably isn't there, by way of a ruined city that no one has ever seen—will be just the thing. If that doesn't steady a chap, I

don't know what will." And he rubbed his big frog-like
hands together as if he were talking of going to a party or a
pantomime. "And now," he added, "let's see how those eels
are getting on."

When the meal came it was delicious and the children
had two large helpings each. At first the Marsh-wiggle
wouldn't believe that they really liked it, and when they
had eaten so much that he had to believe them, he fell back
on saying that it would probably disagree with them horribly. "What's food for wiggles may be poison for humans, I
shouldn't wonder," he said. After the meal they had tea, in
tins (as you've seen men having it who are working on the
road), and Puddleglum had a good many sips out of a
square black bottle. He offered the children some of it, but
they thought it very nasty.

The rest of the day was spent in preparations for an early
start tomorrow morning. Puddleglum, being far the
biggest, said he would carry three blankets, with a large bit
of bacon rolled up inside them. Jill was to carry the remains
of the eels, some biscuit, and the tinder-box. Scrubb was to
carry both his own cloak and Jill's when they didn't want to

wear them. Scrubb (who had learned some shooting when he sailed to the East under Caspian) had Puddleglum's second-best bow, and Puddleglum had his best one; though he said that what with winds, and damp bowstrings, and bad light, and cold fingers, it was a hundred to one against either of them hitting anything. He and Scrubb both had swords—Scrubb had brought the one which had been left out for him in his room at Cair Paravel, but Jill had to be content with her knife. There would have been a quarrel about this, but as soon as they started sparring the wiggle rubbed his hands and said, "Ah, there you are. I thought as much. That's what usually happens on adventures." This made them both shut up.

All three went to bed early in the wigwam. This time the children really had a rather bad night. That was because Puddleglum, after saying, "You'd better try for some sleep, you two; not that I suppose any of us will close an eye tonight," instantly went off into such a loud, continuous snore that, when Jill at last got to sleep, she dreamed all night about road-drills and waterfalls and being in express trains in tunnels.

Chapter Six

The Wild Waste Lands
of the North

AT ABOUT NINE O'CLOCK NEXT MORNING THREE lonely figures might have been seen picking their way across the Shribble by the shoals and stepping-stones. It was a shallow, noisy stream, and even Jill was not wet above her knees when they reached the northern bank. About fifty yards ahead, the land rose up to the beginning of the moor, everywhere steeply, and often in cliffs.

"I suppose *that's* our way!" said Scrubb, pointing left and west to where a stream flowed down from the moor through a shallow gorge. But the Marsh-wiggle shook his head.

"The giants mainly live along the side of that gorge," he said. "You might say the gorge was like a street to them. We'll do better straight ahead, even though it's a bit steep."

They found a place where they could scramble up, and in about ten minutes stood panting at the top. They cast a longing look back at the valley-land of Narnia and then turned their faces to the North. The vast, lonely moor stretched on and up as far as they could see. On their left was rockier ground. Jill thought that must be the edge of the giants' gorge and did not much care about looking in that direction. They set out.

It was good, springy ground for walking, and a day of pale winter sunlight. As they got deeper into the moor, the loneliness increased: one could hear peewits and see an occasional hawk. When they halted in the middle of the morning for a rest and a drink in a little hollow by a stream, Jill was beginning to feel that she might enjoy adventures after all, and said so.

"We haven't had any yet," said the Marsh-wiggle.

Walks after the first halt—like school mornings after break or railway journeys after changing trains—never go on as they were before. When they set out again, Jill noticed that the rocky edge of the gorge had drawn nearer. And the rocks were less flat, more upright, than they had been. In fact they were like little towers of rock. And what funny shapes they were!

"I do believe," thought Jill, "that all the stories about giants might have come from those funny rocks. If you were coming along here when it was half dark, you could easily think those piles of rock were giants. Look at that one, now! You could almost imagine that the lump on top was a head. It would be rather too big for the body, but it would do well enough for an ugly giant. And all that bushy stuff—I suppose it's heather and birds' nests, really—would do quite well for hair and beard. And the things sticking out on each side are quite like ears. They'd be horribly big, but then I daresay giants would have big ears, like elephants. And—o-o-oh!—"

Her blood froze. The thing moved. It was a real giant. There was no mistaking it; she had seen it turn its head.

She had caught a glimpse of the great, stupid, puff-cheeked face. All the things were giants, not rocks. There were forty or fifty of them, all in a row; obviously standing with their feet on the bottom of the gorge and their elbows resting on the edge of the gorge, just as men might stand leaning on a wall—lazy men, on a fine morning after breakfast.

"Keep straight on," whispered Puddleglum, who had noticed them too. "Don't look at them. And whatever you do, don't *run*. They'd all be after us in a moment."

So they kept on, pretending not to have seen the giants. It was like walking past the gate of a house where there is a fierce dog, only far worse. There were dozens and dozens of these giants. They didn't look angry—or kind—or interested at all. There was no sign that they had seen the travelers.

Then—whizz-whizz-whizz—some heavy object came hurtling through the air, and with a crash a big boulder fell about twenty paces ahead of them. And then—thud!—another fell twenty feet behind.

"Are they aiming at us?" asked Scrubb.

"No," said Puddleglum. "We'd be a good deal safer if they were. They're trying to hit *that*—that cairn over there to the right. They won't hit *it*, you know. *It's* safe enough; they're such very bad shots. They play cock-shies most fine mornings. About the only game they're clever enough to understand."

It was a horrible time. There seemed no end of the line of giants, and they never ceased hurling stones, some of which fell extremely close. Quite apart from the real danger, the very sight and sound of their faces and voices were enough to scare anyone. Jill tried not to look at them.

After about twenty-five minutes the giants apparently had a quarrel. This put an end to the cock-shies, but it is not pleasant to be within a mile of quarreling giants. They stormed and jeered at one another in long, meaningless words of about twenty syllables each. They foamed and gibbered and jumped in their rage, and each jump shook the earth like a bomb. They lammed each other on the head with great, clumsy stone hammers; but their skulls were so hard that the hammers bounced off again, and then the monster who had given the blow would drop his hammer and howl with pain because it had stung his fingers. But he was so stupid that he would do exactly the same thing a minute later. This was a good thing in the long run, for by the end of an hour all the giants were so hurt that they sat down and began to cry. When they sat down, their heads were below the edge of the gorge, so that you saw them no more; but Jill could hear them howling and blubbering and boo-hooing like great babies even after the place was a mile behind.

That night they bivouacked on the bare moor, and Puddleglum showed the children how to make the best of their blankets by sleeping back to back. (The backs keep each other warm and you can then have both blankets on top.) But it was chilly even so, and the ground was hard and lumpy. The Marsh-wiggle told them they would feel more comfortable if only they thought how very much colder it would be later on and farther north; but this didn't cheer them up at all.

They traveled across Ettinsmoor for many days, saving the bacon and living chiefly on the moor-fowl (they were not, of course, *talking* birds) which Eustace and the wiggle shot. Jill rather envied Eustace for being able to shoot; he had learned it on his voyage with King Caspian. As there were countless streams on the moor, they were never short of water. Jill thought that when, in books, people live on what they shoot, it never tells you what a long, smelly, messy job it is plucking and cleaning dead birds, and how cold it makes your fingers. But the great thing was that they met hardly any giants. One giant saw them, but he only roared with laughter and stumped away about his own business.

About the tenth day, they reached a place where the country changed. They came to the northern edge of the moor and looked down a long, steep slope into a different, and grimmer, land. At the bottom of the slope were cliffs: beyond these, a country of high mountains, dark precipices, stony valleys, ravines so deep and narrow that one could not see far into them, and rivers that poured out of echoing gorges to plunge sullenly into black depths. Needless to say, it was Puddleglum who pointed out a sprinkling of snow on the more distant slopes.

"But there'll be more on the north side of them, I shouldn't wonder," he added.

It took them some time to reach the foot of the slope and, when they did, they looked down from the top of the cliffs at a river running below them from west to east. It was walled in by precipices on the far side as well as on their own, and it was green and sunless, full of rapids and water-falls. The roar of it shook the earth even where they stood.

"The bright side of it is," said Puddleglum, "that if we break our necks getting down the cliff, then we're safe from being drowned in the river."

"What about *that*?" said Scrubb suddenly, pointing upstream to their left. Then they all looked and saw the last thing they were expecting—a bridge. And what a bridge, too! It was a huge, single arch that spanned the gorge from cliff-top to cliff-top; and the crown of that arch was as high above the cliff-tops as the dome of St. Paul's is above the street.

"Why, it must be a giants' bridge!" said Jill.

"Or a sorcerer's, more likely," said Puddleglum. "We've got to look out for enchantments in a place like this. I think it's a trap. I think it'll turn into mist and melt away just when we're out on the middle of it."

"Oh, for goodness' sake, don't be such a wet blanket," said Scrubb. "Why on earth shouldn't it be a proper bridge?"

"Do you think any of the giants we've seen would have sense to build a thing like that?" said Puddleglum.

"But mightn't it have been built by other giants?" said Jill. "I mean, by giants who lived hundreds of years ago, and were far cleverer than the modern kind. It might have been built by the same ones who built the giant city we're looking for. And that would mean we were on the right track—the old bridge leading to the old city!"

"That's a real brain-wave, Pole," said Scrubb. "It must be that. Come on."

So they turned and went to the bridge. And when they reached it, it certainly seemed solid enough. The single stones were as big as those at Stonehenge and must have been squared by good masons once, though now they were cracked and crumbled. The balustrade had apparently been covered with rich carvings, of which some traces remained; mouldering faces and forms of giants, minotaurs, squids, centipedes, and dreadful gods. Puddleglum still didn't trust it, but he consented to cross it with the children.

The climb up to the crown of the arch was long and heavy. In many places the great stones had dropped out, leaving horrible gaps through which you looked down on the river foaming thousands of feet below. They saw an eagle fly through under their feet. And the higher they went, the colder it grew, and the wind blew so that they could hardly keep their footing. It seemed to shake the bridge.

When they reached the top and could look down the farther slope of the bridge, they saw what looked like the remains of an ancient giant road stretching away before them into the heart of the mountains. Many stones of its pavement were missing and there were wide patches of grass between those that remained. And riding toward them on that ancient road were two people of normal grown-up human size.

"Keep on. Move toward them," said Puddleglum. "Anyone you meet in a place like this is as likely as not to be an enemy, but we mustn't let them think we're afraid."

By the time they had stepped off the end of the bridge onto the grass, the two strangers were quite close. One was a knight in complete armor with his visor down. His armor and his horse were black; there was no device on his shield and no banneret on his spear. The other was a lady on a white horse, a horse so lovely that you wanted to kiss its nose and give it a lump of sugar at once. But the lady, who rode side-saddle and wore a long, fluttering dress of dazzling green, was lovelier still.

"Good day, t-r-r-avelers," she cried out in a voice as sweet as the sweetest bird's song, trilling her R's delightfully. "Some of you are young pilgrims to walk this rough waste."

"That's as may be, Ma'am," said Puddleglum very stiffly and on his guard.

"We're looking for the ruined city of the giants," said Jill.

"The r-r-ruined city?" said the Lady. "That is a strange place to be seeking. What will you do if you find it?"

"We've got to—" began Jill, but Puddleglum interrupted.

"Begging your pardon, ma'am. But we don't know you or your friend—a silent chap, isn't he?—and you don't know us. And we'd as soon not talk to strangers about our business, if you don't mind. Shall we have a little rain soon, do you think?"

The Lady laughed: the richest, most musical laugh you can imagine. "Well, children," she said, "you have a wise, solemn old guide with you. I think none the worse of him for keeping his own counsel, but I'll be free with mine. I have often heard the name of the giantish City Ruinous, but never met any who would tell me the way thither. This road leads to the burgh and castle of Harfang, where dwell the gentle giants. They are as mild, civil, prudent, and courteous as those of Ettinsmoor are foolish, fierce, savage, and given to all beastliness. And in Harfang you may or may not hear tidings of the City Ruinous, but certainly you shall find good lodgings and merry hosts. You would be wise to winter there, or, at the least, to tarry certain days for your ease and refreshment. There you shall have steaming baths, soft beds, and bright hearths; and the roast and the baked and the sweet and the strong will be on the table four times a day."

"I say!" exclaimed Scrubb. "That's something like! Think of sleeping in a bed again."

"Yes, and having a hot bath," said Jill. "Do you think they'll ask us to stay? We don't know them, you see."

"Only tell them," answered the Lady, "that She of the Green Kirtle salutes them by you, and has sent them two fair Southern children for the Autumn Feast."

"Oh, thank you, thank you ever so much," said Jill and Scrubb.

"But have a care," said the Lady. "On whatever day you reach Harfang, that you come not to the door too late. For they shut their gates a few hours after noon, and it is the custom of the castle that they open to none when once they have drawn bolt, how hard so ever he knock."

The children thanked her again, with shining eyes, and the Lady waved to them. The Marsh-wiggle took off his steeple-hat and bowed very stiffly. Then the silent Knight and the Lady started walking their horses up the slope of the bridge with a great clatter of hoofs.

"Well!" said Puddleglum. "I'd give a good deal to know where *she's* coming from and where she's going. Not the sort you expect to meet in the wilds of Giantland, is she? Up to no good, I'll be bound."

"Oh rot!" said Scrubb. "I thought she was simply super. And think of hot meals and warm rooms. I do hope Harfang isn't a long way off."

"Same here," said Jill. "And hadn't she a scrumptious dress? And the horse!"

"All the same," said Puddleglum, "I wish we knew a bit more about her."

"I *was* going to ask her all about herself," said Jill. "But how could I when you wouldn't tell her anything about us?"

"Yes," said Scrubb. "And why were you so stiff and unpleasant? Didn't you like them?"

"Them?" said the wiggle. "Who's *them*? I only saw one."

"Didn't you see the Knight?" asked Jill.

"I saw a suit of armor," said Puddleglum. "Why didn't he speak?"

"I expect he was shy," said Jill. "Or perhaps he just wants

to look at her and listen to her lovely voice. I'm sure I would if I was him."

"I was wondering," remarked Puddleglum, "what you'd really see if you lifted up the visor of that helmet and looked inside."

"Hang it all," said Scrubb. "Think of the shape of the armor! What *could* be inside it except a man?"

"How about a skeleton?" asked the Marsh-wiggle with ghastly cheerfulness. "Or perhaps," he added as an after-thought, "nothing at all. I mean, nothing you could see. Someone invisible."

"Really, Puddleglum," said Jill with a shudder, "you do have the most horrible ideas. How do you think of them all?"

"Oh, bother his ideas!" said Scrubb. "He's always expecting the worst, and he's always wrong. Let's think about those Gentle Giants and get on to Harfang as quickly as we can. I wish I knew how far it is."

And now they nearly had the first of those quarrels which Puddleglum had foretold: not that Jill and Scrubb hadn't been sparring and snapping at each other a good deal before, but this was the first really serious disagreement. Puddleglum didn't want them to go to Harfang at all. He said that he didn't know what a giant's idea of being "gentle" might be, and that, anyway, Aslan's signs had said nothing about staying with giants, gentle or otherwise. The children, on the other hand, who were sick of wind and rain, and skinny fowl roasted over campfires, and hard, cold earth to sleep on, were absolutely dead set to visit the Gentle Giants. In the end, Puddleglum agreed to do so, but only on one condition. The others must give an absolute promise that, unless he gave them leave, they would not tell the Gentle Giants that they came from Narnia or that they were looking for Prince Rilian. And they gave him this promise, and went on.

After that talk with the Lady things got worse in two different ways. In the first place the country was much harder. The road led through endless, narrow valleys down which a cruel north wind was always blowing in their faces. There was nothing that could be used for firewood, and there were no nice little hollows to camp in, as there had been on the moor. And the ground was all stony, and made your feet sore by day and every bit of you sore by night.

In the second place, whatever the Lady had intended by telling them about Harfang, the actual effect on the children was a bad one. They could think about nothing but beds and baths and hot meals and how lovely it would be to get indoors. They never talked about Aslan, or even about the lost prince, now. And Jill gave up her habit of repeating the signs over to herself every night and morning. She said to herself, at first, that she was too tired, but she soon forgot all about it. And though you might have expected that the idea of having a good time at Harfang would have made them more cheerful, it really made them more sorry for themselves and more grumpy and snappy with each other and with Puddleglum.

At last they came one afternoon to a place where the gorge in which they were traveling widened out and dark fir woods rose on either side. They looked ahead and saw that they had come through the mountains. Before them lay a desolate, rocky plain: beyond it, further mountains capped with snow. But between them and those further mountains rose a low hill with an irregular flattish top.

"Look! Look!" cried Jill, and pointed across the plain; and there, through the gathering dusk, from beyond the flat hill, everyone saw lights. Lights! Not moonlight, nor fires, but a homely cheering row of lighted windows. If you have never been in the wild wilderness, day and night, for weeks, you will hardly understand how they felt.

"Harfang!" cried Scrubb and Jill in glad, excited voices; and, "Harfang," repeated Puddleglum in a dull, gloomy voice. But he added, "Hullo! Wild geese!" and had the bow off his shoulder in a second. He brought down a good fat goose. It was far too late to think of reaching Harfang that day. But they had a hot meal and a fire, and started the night warmer than they had been for over a week. After the fire had gone out, the night grew bitterly cold, and when they woke next morning, their blankets were stiff with frost.

"Never mind!" said Jill, stamping her feet. "Hot baths tonight!"

Chapter Seven

The Hill of the Strange Trenches

THERE IS NO DENYING IT WAS A BEAST OF A DAY. Overhead was a sunless sky, muffled in clouds that were heavy with snow; underfoot, a black frost; blowing over it, a wind that felt as if it would take your skin off. When they got down into the plain they found that this part of the ancient road was much more ruinous than any they had yet seen. They had to pick their way over great broken stones and between boulders and across rubble: hard going for sore feet. And, however tired they got, it was far too cold for a halt.

At about ten o'clock the first tiny snow flakes came loitering down and settled on Jill's arm. Ten minutes later they were falling quite thickly. In twenty minutes the ground was noticeably white. And by the end of half an hour a good steady snowstorm, which looked as if it meant to last all day, was driving in their faces so that they could hardly see.

In order to understand what followed, you must keep on remembering how little they could see. As they drew near the low hill which separated them from the place where the lighted windows had appeared, they had no general view of it at all. It was a question of seeing the next few paces ahead, and, even for that, you had to screw up your eyes. Needless to say, they were not talking.

When they reached the foot of the hill they caught a glimpse of what might be rocks on each side—squarish rocks, if you looked at them carefully, but no one did. All were more concerned with the ledge right in front of them which barred their way. It was about four feet high. The

Marsh-wiggle, with his long legs, had no difficulty in jumping onto the top of it, and he then helped the others up. It was a nasty wet business for them, though not for him, because the snow now lay quite deep on the ledge. They then had a stiff climb—Jill fell once—up very rough ground for about a hundred yards, and came to a second ledge. There were four of these ledges altogether, at quite irregular intervals.

As they struggled onto the fourth ledge, there was no mistaking the fact that they were now at the top of the flat hill. Up till now the slope had given them some shelter; here, they got the full fury of the wind. For the hill, oddly enough, was quite as flat on top as it had looked from a distance: a great level tableland which the storm tore across without resistance. In most places the snow was still hardly lying at all, for the wind kept catching it up off the ground in sheets and clouds, and hurling it in their faces. And round their feet little eddies of snow ran about as you sometimes see them doing over ice. And, indeed, in many places, the surface was almost as smooth as ice. But to make matters worse it was crossed and crisscrossed with curious banks or dikes, which sometimes divided it up into squares and oblongs. All these of course had to be climbed; they varied from two to five feet in height and were about a couple of yards thick. On the north side of each bank the snow already lay in deep drifts; and after each climb you came down into the drift and got wet.

Fighting her way forward with hood up and head down and numb hands inside her cloak, Jill had glimpses of other odd things on that horrible tableland—things on her right that looked vaguely like factory chimneys, and, on her left, a huge cliff, straighter than any cliff ought to be. But she wasn't at all interested and didn't give them a thought. The only things she thought about were her cold hands (and nose and chin and ears) and hot baths and beds at Harfang.

Suddenly she skidded, slid about five feet, and found herself to her horror sliding down into a dark, narrow chasm which seemed that moment to have appeared in front of her. Half a second later she had reached the bottom. She appeared to be in a kind of trench or groove, only about three feet wide. And though she was shaken by the fall, almost the first thing she noticed was the relief of being out of the wind; for the walls of the trench rose high above her. The next thing she noticed was, naturally, the anxious faces of Scrubb and Puddleglum looking down at her from the edge.

"Are you hurt, Pole?" shouted Scrubb.

"*Both* legs broken, I shouldn't wonder," shouted Puddleglum.

Jill stood up and explained that she was all right, but they'd have to help her out.

"What is it you've fallen into?" asked Scrubb.

"It's a kind of trench, or it might be a kind of sunken lane or something," said Jill. "It runs quite straight."

"Yes, by Jove," said Scrubb. "And it runs due north! I wonder, is it a sort of road? If it was, we'd be out of this infernal wind down there. Is there a lot of snow at the bottom?"

"Hardly any. It all blows over the top, I suppose."

"What happens farther on?"

"Half a sec. I'll go and see," said Jill. She got up and walked along the trench; but before she had gone far, it turned sharply to the right. She shouted this information back to the others.

"What's round the corner?" asked Scrubb.

Now it happened that Jill had the same feeling about twisty passages and dark places underground, or even nearly underground, that Scrubb had about the edges of cliffs. She had no intention of going round that corner alone; especially when she heard Puddleglum bawling out from behind her:

"Be careful, Pole. It's just the sort of place that might lead to a dragon's cave. And in a giant country, there might be giant earth-worms or giant beetles."

"I don't think it goes anywhere much," said Jill, coming hastily back.

"I'm jolly well going to have a look," said Scrubb. "What do you mean by *anywhere much*, I should like to know?" So he sat down on the edge of the trench (everyone was too wet by now to bother about being a bit wetter) and then dropped in. He pushed past Jill and, though he didn't say anything, she felt sure that he knew she had funked it. So she followed him closely, but took care not to get in front of him.

It proved, however, to be a disappointing exploration.

They went round the right-hand turn and straight on for a few paces. Here there was a choice of ways: straight on again, or sharp to the right. "That's no good," said Scrubb glancing down the right-hand turn, "that would be taking us back—south." He went straight on, but once more, in a few steps, they found a second turn to the right. But this time there was no choice of ways, for the trench they had been following here came to a dead end.

"No good," grunted Scrubb. Jill lost no time in turning and leading the way back. When they returned to the place where Jill had first fallen in, the Marsh-wiggle with his long arms had no difficulty in pulling them out.

But it was dreadful to be out on top again. Down in those narrow slits of trenches, their ears had almost begun to thaw. They had been able to see clearly and breathe easily and hear each other speak without shouting. It was absolute misery to come back into the withering coldness. And it did seem hard when Puddleglum chose that moment for saying:

"Are you still sure of those signs, Pole? What's the one we ought to be after now?"

"Oh, come on! Bother the signs," said Pole. "Something about someone mentioning Aslan's name, I think. But I'm jolly well not going to give a recitation here."

As you see, she had got the order wrong. That was because she had given up saying the signs over every night. She still really knew them, if she troubled to think: but she was no longer so "pat" in her lesson as to be sure of reeling them off in the right order at a moment's notice and without thinking. Puddleglum's question annoyed her because, deep down inside her, she was already annoyed with herself for not knowing the Lion's lesson quite so well as she felt she ought to have known it. This annoyance, added to the misery of being very cold and tired, made her say, "Bother the signs." She didn't perhaps quite mean it.

"Oh, that was next, was it?" said Puddleglum. "Now I wonder, are you right? Got 'em mixed, I shouldn't wonder. It seems to me, this hill, this flat place we're on, is worth stopping to have a look at. Have you noticed—"

"Oh, Lor!" said Scrubb, "is this a time for stopping to admire the view? For goodness' sake let's get on."

"Oh, look, look, look," cried Jill and pointed. Everyone

turned, and everyone saw. Some way off to the north, and a good deal higher up than the tableland on which they stood, a line of lights had appeared. This time, even more obviously than when the travelers had seen them the night before, they were windows: smaller windows that made one think deliciously of bedrooms, and larger windows that made one think of great halls with fires roaring on the hearth and hot soup or juicy sirloins smoking on the table.

"Harfang!" exclaimed Scrubb.

"That's all very well," said Puddleglum. "But what I was saying was—"

"Oh, shut up," said Jill crossly. "We haven't a moment to lose. Don't you remember what the Lady said about their locking up so early? We must get there in time, we must, we must. We'll *die* if we're shut out on a night like this."

"Well, it isn't exactly a night, not yet," began Puddleglum; but the two children both said, "Come on," and began stumbling forward on the slippery tableland as quickly as their legs would carry them. The Marsh-wiggle followed them: still talking, but now that they were forcing

their way into the wind again, they could not have heard
him even if they had wanted to. And they didn't want.
They were thinking of baths and beds and hot drinks; and
the idea of coming to Harfang too late and being shut out
was almost unbearable.

In spite of their haste, it took them a long time to cross
the flat top of that hill. And even when they had crossed it,
there were still several ledges to climb down on the far side.
But at last they reached the bottom and could see what
Harfang was like.

It stood on a high crag, and in spite of its many towers
was more a huge house than a castle. Obviously, the
Gentle Giants feared no attack. There were windows in
the outside wall quite close to the ground—a thing no
one would have in a serious fortress. There were even odd
little doors here and there, so that it would be quite easy
to get in and out of the castle without going through the
courtyard. This raised the spirits of Jill and Scrubb. It
made the whole place look more friendly and less forbid-
ding.

At first the height and steepness of the crag frightened

them, but presently they noticed that there was an easier way up on the left and that the road wound up toward it. It was a terrible climb, after the journey they had already had, and Jill nearly gave up. Scrubb and Puddleglum had to help her for the last hundred yards. But in the end they stood before the castle gate. The portcullis was up and the gate was open.

However tired you are, it takes some nerve to walk up to a giant's front door. In spite of all his previous warnings against Harfang, it was Puddleglum who showed the most courage.

"Steady pace, now," he said. "Don't look frightened, whatever you do. We've done the silliest thing in the world by coming at all: but now that we *are* here, we'd best put a bold face on it."

With these words he strode forward into the gateway, stood still under the arch where the echo would help his voice, and called out as loud as he could.

"Ho! Porter! Guests who seek lodging."

And while he was waiting for something to happen, he took off his hat and knocked off the heavy mass of snow which had gathered on its wide brim.

"I say," whispered Scrubb to Jill. "He may be a wet blanket, but he has plenty of pluck—and cheek."

A door opened, letting out a delicious glow of firelight, and the Porter appeared. Jill bit her lips for fear she should scream. He was not a perfectly enormous giant; that is to say, he was rather taller than an apple tree but nothing like so tall as a telegraph pole. He had bristly red hair, a leather jerkin with metal plates fastened all over it so as to make a kind of mail shirt, bare knees (very hairy indeed) and things like puttees on his legs. He stooped down and goggled at Puddleglum.

"And what sort of creature do you call yourself," he said.

Jill took her courage in both hands. "Please," she said, shouting up to the giant. "The Lady of the Green Kirtle salutes the King of the Gentle Giants, and has sent us two Southern children and this Marsh-wiggle (his name's Puddleglum) to your Autumn Feast.—If it's quite convenient, of course," she added.

"O-ho!" said the Porter. "That's quite a different story.

Come in, little people, come in. You'd best come into the lodge while I'm sending word to his Majesty." He looked at the children with curiosity. "Blue faces," he said. "I didn't know they were that color. Don't care about it myself. But I dare say you look quite nice to one another. Beetles fancy other beetles, they do say."

"Our faces are only blue with cold," said Jill. "We're not this color *really*."

"Then come in and get warm. Come in, little shrimps," said the Porter. They followed him into the lodge. And though it was rather terrible to hear such a big door clang shut behind them, they forgot about it as soon as they saw the thing they had been longing for ever since supper time last night—a fire. And such a fire! It looked as if four or five whole trees were blazing on it, and it was so hot they couldn't go within yards of it. But they all flopped down on the brick floor, as near as they could bear the heat, and heaved great sighs of relief.

"Now, youngster," said the Porter to another giant who had been sitting in the back of the room, staring at the visitors till it looked as if his eyes would start out of

his head, "run across with this message to the House."
And he repeated what Jill had said to him. The younger
giant, after a final stare, and a great guffaw, left the room.

"Now, Froggy," said the Porter to Puddleglum, "you
look as if you wanted some cheering up." He produced a
black bottle very like Puddleglum's own, but about
twenty times larger. "Let me see, let me see," said the Porter.
"I can't give you a cup or you'll drown yourself. Let me see.
This salt-cellar will be just the thing. You needn't mention
it over at the House. The silver *will* keep on getting over
here, and it's not my fault."

The salt-cellar was not very like one of ours, being
narrower and more upright, and made quite a good cup
for Puddleglum, when the giant set it down on the floor
beside him. The children expected Puddleglum to refuse
it, distrusting the Gentle Giants as he did. But he muttered, "It's rather late to be thinking of precautions now
that we're inside and the door shut behind us." Then he
sniffed at the liquor. "Smells all right," he said. "But that's
nothing to go by. Better make sure," and took a sip. "Tastes
all right, too," he said. "But it might do that at the *first* sip.

How does it go on?" He took a larger sip. "Ah!" he said. "But is it the same all the way down?" and took another. "There'll be something nasty at the bottom, I shouldn't wonder," he said, and finished the drink. He licked his lips and remarked to the children, "This'll be a test, you see. If I curl up, or burst, or turn into a lizard, or something, then you'll know not to take anything they offer you." But the giant, who was too far up to hear the things Puddleglum had been saying under his breath, roared with laughter and said, "Why, Froggy, you're a man. See him put it away!"

"Not a man ... Marsh-wiggle," replied Puddleglum in a somewhat indistinct voice. "Not frog, either: Marsh-wiggle."

At that moment the door opened behind them and the younger giant came in saying, "They're to go to the throne-room at once."

The children stood up but Puddleglum remained sitting and said, "Marsh-wiggle. Marsh-wiggle. Very respectable Marsh-wiggle. Respectowiggle."

"Show them the way, young 'un," said the giant Porter.

"You'd better carry Froggy. He's had a drop more than's good for him."

"Nothing wrong with me," said Puddleglum. "Not a frog. Nothing frog with me. I'm a respectabiggle."

But the young giant caught him up by the waist and signed to the children to follow. In this undignified way they crossed the courtyard. Puddleglum, held in the giant's fist, and vaguely kicking the air, did certainly look very like a frog. But they had little time to notice this, for they soon entered the great doorway of the main castle— both their hearts were beating faster than usual—and, after pattering along several corridors at a trot to keep up with the giant's paces, found themselves blinking in the light of an enormous room, where lamps glowed and fire roared on the hearth and both were reflected from the gilding of roof and cornice. More giants than they could count stood on their left and right, all in magnificent robes; and on two thrones at the far end, sat two huge shapes that appeared to be the King and Queen.

About twenty feet from the thrones, they stopped. Scrubb and Jill made an awkward attempt at a bow (girls are not taught how to curtsey at Experiment House) and the young giant carefully put Puddleglum down on the floor, where he collapsed into a sort of sitting position. With his long limbs he looked, to tell the truth, uncommonly like a large spider.

Chapter Eight

The House of Harfang

"GO ON, POLE, DO YOUR STUFF," WHISPERED SCRUBB.

Jill found that her mouth was so dry that she couldn't speak a word. She nodded savagely at Scrubb.

Thinking to himself that he would never forgive her (or Puddleglum either), Scrubb licked his lips and shouted up to the King giant.

"If you please, Sire, the Lady of the Green Kirtle salutes you by us and said you'd like to have us for your Autumn Feast."

The giant King and Queen looked at each other, nodded to each other, and smiled in a way that Jill didn't exactly like. She liked the King better than the Queen. He had a fine, curled beard and a straight eagle-like nose, and was really rather good-looking as giants go. The Queen was dreadfully fat and had a double chin and a fat, powdered face—which isn't a very nice thing at the best of times, and of course looks much worse when it is ten times too big. Then the King put out his tongue and licked his lips. Anyone might do that; but his tongue was so very large and red, and came out so unexpectedly, that it gave Jill quite a shock.

"Oh, what *good* children!" said the Queen. ("Perhaps she's the nice one after all," thought Jill.)

"Yes indeed," said the King. "Quite excellent children. We welcome you to our court. Give me your hands."

He stretched down his great right hand—very clean and with any number of rings on the fingers, but also with terrible pointed nails. He was much too big to shake the hands which the children, in turn, held up to him; but he shook the arms.

"And what's *that?*" asked the King, pointing to Puddleglum.

"Reshpeckobiggle," said Puddleglum.

"Oh!" screamed the Queen, gathering her skirts close about her ankles. "The horrid thing! It's alive."

"He's quite all right, your Majesty, really, he is," said Scrubb hastily. "You'll like him much better when you get to know him. I'm sure you will."

I hope you won't lose all interest in Jill for the rest of the book if I tell you that at this moment she began to cry. There was a good deal of excuse for her. Her feet and hands and ears and nose were still only just beginning to thaw; melted snow was trickling off her clothes; she had had hardly anything to eat or drink that day; and her legs were aching so that she felt she could not go on standing much longer. Anyway, it did more good at the moment than anything else would have done, for the Queen said:

"Ah, the poor child! My lord, we do wrong to keep our guests standing. Quick, some of you! Take them away. Give them food and wine and baths. Comfort the little girl. Give her lollipops, give her dolls, give her physics, give her all you can think of—possets and comfits and caraways and lullabies and toys. Don't cry, little girl, or you won't be good for anything when the feast comes."

Jill was just as indignant as you and I would have been at the mention of toys and dolls; and, though lollipops and comfits might be all very well in their way, she very much hoped that something more solid would be provided. The Queen's foolish speech, however, produced excellent results, for Puddleglum and Scrubb were at once picked up by gigantic gentlemen-in-waiting, and Jill by a gigantic maid of honor, and carried off to their rooms.

Jill's room was about the size of a church, and would have been rather grim if it had not had a roaring fire on the hearth and a very thick crimson carpet on the floor. And here delightful things began to happen to her. She was handed over to the Queen's old Nurse, who was, from the giants' point of view, a little old woman almost bent double with age, and, from the human point of view, a giantess small enough to go about an ordinary room without knocking her head on the ceiling. She was very capable, though Jill did wish she wouldn't keep on clicking her tongue and saying things like "Oh, la, la! Ups-a-daisy" and "There's a duck" and "Now we'll be all right, my poppet." She filled a giant foot-bath with hot water and helped Jill into it. If you can swim (as Jill could) a giant bath is a lovely thing. And giant towels, though a bit rough and coarse, are lovely too, because there are acres of them. In fact you don't need to dry at all, you just roll about on them in front of the fire and enjoy yourself. And when that was over, clean, fresh, warmed clothes were put on Jill, very splendid clothes and a little too big for her, but clearly made for humans not giantesses. "I suppose if that woman in the green kirtle comes here, they must be used to guests of our size," thought Jill.

She soon saw that she was right about this, for a table and chair of the right height for an ordinary grown-up human were placed for her, and the knives and forks and spoons were the proper size too. It was delightful to sit down, feeling warm and clean at last. Her feet were still bare and it was lovely to tread on the giant carpet. She sank in it well over her ankles and it was just the thing for sore feet. The meal—which I suppose we must call dinner, though it was nearer tea time—was cock-a-leekie soup, and hot roast turkey, and a steamed pudding, and roast chestnuts, and as much fruit as you could eat.

The only annoying thing was that the Nurse kept coming in and out, and every time she came in, she brought a gigantic toy with her—a huge doll, bigger than Jill herself, a wooden horse on wheels, about the size of an elephant, a drum that looked like a young gasometer, and a woolly lamb. They were crude, badly made things, painted in very bright colors, and Jill hated the sight of them. She kept on telling the Nurse she didn't want them, but the Nurse said:

"Tut-tut-tut-tut. You'll want 'em all right when you've had a bit of a rest, I know! Te-he-he! Beddy bye, now. A precious poppet!"

The bed was not a giant bed but only a big four-poster, like what you might see in an old-fashioned hotel; and very small it looked in that enormous room. She was very glad to tumble into it.

"Is it still snowing, Nurse?" she asked sleepily.

"No. Raining now, ducky!" said the giantess. "Rain'll

wash away all the nasty snow. Precious poppet will be able to go out and play tomorrow!" And she tucked Jill up and said good night.

I know nothing so disagreeable as being kissed by a giantess. Jill thought the same, but was asleep in five minutes.

The rain fell steadily all the evening and all the night, dashing against the windows of the castle, and Jill never heard it but slept deeply, past supper time and past midnight. And then came the deadest hour of the night and nothing stirred but mice in the house of the giants. At that hour there came to Jill a dream. It seemed to her that she awoke in the same room and saw the fire, sunk low and red, and in the firelight the great wooden horse. And the horse came of its own will, rolling on its wheels across the carpet, and stood at her head. And now it was no longer a horse, but a lion as big as the horse. And then it was not a toy lion, but a real lion, The Real Lion, just as she had seen him on the mountain beyond the world's end. And a smell of all sweet-smelling things there are filled the room. But there was some trouble in Jill's mind, though she could not

think what it was, and the tears streamed down her face
and wet the pillow. The Lion told her to repeat the signs,
and she found that she had forgotten them all. At that, a
great horror came over her. And Aslan took her up in his
jaws (she could feel his lips and his breath but not his
teeth) and carried her to the window and made her look
out. The moon shone bright; and written in great letters
across the world or the sky (she did not know which) were
the words UNDER ME. After that, the dream faded away,
and when she woke, very late next morning, she did not
remember that she had dreamed at all.

She was up and dressed and had finished breakfast in
front of the fire when the Nurse opened the door and said:
"Here's pretty poppet's little friends come to play with
her."

In came Scrubb and the Marsh-wiggle.

"Hullo! Good morning," said Jill. "Isn't this fun? I've
slept about fifteen hours, I believe. I do feel better, don't
you?"

"I do," said Scrubb, "but Puddleglum says he has a
headache. Hullo!—your window has a window seat. If we

got up on that, we could see out." And at once they all did so: and at the first glance Jill said, "Oh, how perfectly dreadful!"

The sun was shining and, except for a few drifts, the snow had been almost completely washed away by the rain. Down below them, spread out like a map, lay the flat hill-top which they had struggled over yesterday afternoon; seen from the castle, it could not be mistaken for anything but the ruins of a gigantic city. It had been flat, as Jill now saw, because it was still, on the whole, paved, though in places the pavement was broken. The criss-cross banks were what was left of the walls of huge buildings which might once have been giants' palaces and temples. One bit of wall, about five hundred feet high, was still standing; it was that which she had thought was a cliff. The things that had looked like factory chimneys were enormous pillars, broken off at unequal heights; their fragments lay at their bases like felled trees of monstrous stone. The ledges which they had climbed down on the north side of the hill—and also, no doubt the other ledges which they had climbed up on the south side—were the remaining steps of giant stairs. To crown all, in large, dark lettering across the center of the pavement, ran the words UNDER ME.

The three travelers looked at each other in dismay, and, after a short whistle, Scrubb said what they were all thinking, "The second and third signs muffed." And at that moment Jill's dream rushed back into her mind.

"It's my fault," she said in despairing tones. "I—I'd given up repeating the signs every night. If I'd been thinking about them I could have seen it was the city, even *in* all that snow."

"I'm worse," said Puddleglum. "I *did* see, or nearly. I thought it looked uncommonly like a ruined city."

"You're the only one who isn't to blame," said Scrubb. "You *did* try to make us stop."

"Didn't try hard enough, though," said the Marsh-wiggle. "And I'd no call to be trying. I ought to have done it. As if I couldn't have stopped you two with one hand each!"

"The truth is," said Scrubb, "we were so jolly keen on getting to this place that we weren't bothering about anything else. At least I know I was. Ever since we met the woman with the knight who didn't talk, we've been thinking of nothing else. We'd nearly forgotten about Prince Rilian."

"I shouldn't wonder," said Puddleglum, "if that wasn't exactly what she intended."

"What I don't quite understand," said Jill, "is how we didn't see the lettering? Or could it have come there since last night. Could he—Aslan—have put it there in the night? I had such a queer dream." And she told them all about it.

"Why, you chump!" said Scrubb. "We did see it. We got into the lettering. Don't you see? We got into the letter E in ME. That was your sunk lane. We walked along the bottom stroke of the E, due north—turned to our right along the upright—came to another turn to the right— that's the middle stroke—and then went on to the top left-hand corner, or (if you like) the northeastern corner of the letter, and came back. Like the bally idiots that we are." He kicked the window seat savagely, and went on, "So it's no good, Pole. I know what you were thinking because I was thinking the same. You were thinking how nice it would have been if Aslan hadn't put the instructions on the stones of the ruined city till after we'd passed it. And then it would have been his fault, not ours. So likely, isn't it? No. We must just own up. We've only four signs to go by, and we've muffed the first three."

"You mean I have," said Jill. "It's quite true. I've spoiled everything ever since you brought me here. All the same— I'm frightfully sorry and all that—all the same, what *are* the instructions? UNDER ME doesn't seem to make much sense."

"Yes it does, though," said Puddleglum. "It means we've got to look for the Prince under that city."

"But how can we?" asked Jill.

"That's the question," said Puddleglum, rubbing his big, frog-like hands together. "How can we *now*? No doubt, if we'd had our minds on our job when we were at the Ruinous City, we'd have been shown how—found a little door, or a cave, or a tunnel, met someone to help us. Might have been (you never know) Aslan himself. We'd have got down under those paving-stones somehow or other. Aslan's instructions always work: there are no exceptions. But how to do it *now*—that's another matter."

"Well, we shall just have to go back, I suppose," said Jill.

"Easy, isn't it?" said Puddleglum. "We might try open-ing that door to begin with." And they all looked at the door and saw that none of them could reach the handle, and that almost certainly no one could turn it if they did.

"Do you think they won't let us out if we ask?" said Jill. And nobody said, but everyone thought, "Supposing they don't."

It was not a pleasant idea. Puddleglum was dead against any idea of telling the giants their real business and simply asking to be let out; and of course the children couldn't tell without his permission, because they had promised. And all three felt pretty sure that there would be no chance of escaping from the castle by night. Once they were in their rooms with the doors shut, they would be prisoners till morning. They might, of course, ask to have their doors left open, but that would rouse suspicions.

"Our only chance," said Scrubb, "is to try to sneak away by daylight. Mightn't there be an hour in the afternoon when most of the giants are asleep?—and if we could steal down into the kitchen, mightn't there be a back door open?"

"It's hardly what I call a Chance," said the Marsh-wiggle. "But it's all the chance we're likely to get." As a matter of fact, Scrubb's plan was not quite so hopeless as you might think. If you want to get out of a house without being seen, the middle of the afternoon is in some ways a better time to try it than the middle of the night. Doors and windows are more likely to be open; and if you *are* caught, you can always pretend you weren't meaning to go far and had no particular plans. (It is very hard to make either giants or grown-ups believe this if you're found climbing out of a bedroom window at one o'clock in the morning.)

"We must put them off their guard, though," said Scrubb. "We must pretend we love being here and are long-ing for this Autumn Feast."

"That's tomorrow night," said Puddleglum. "I heard one of them say so."

"I see," said Jill. "We must pretend to be awfully excited about it, and keep on asking questions. They think we're absolute infants anyway, which will make it easier."

"Gay," said Puddleglum with a deep sigh. "That's what we've got to be. Gay. As if we hadn't a care in the world. Frolicsome. You two youngsters haven't always got very high spirits, I've noticed. You must watch me, and do as I do. I'll be gay. Like this"—and he assumed a ghastly grin. "And frolicsome"—here he cut a most mournful caper. "You'll soon get into it, if you keep your eyes on me. They think I'm a funny fellow already, you see. I dare say you two thought I was a trifle tipsy last night, but I do assure you it was—well, most of it was—put on. I had an idea it would come in useful, somehow."

The children, when they talked over their adventures afterward, could never feel sure whether this last statement was quite strictly true; but they were sure that Puddleglum thought it was true when he made it.

"All right. Gay's the word," said Scrubb. "Now, if we could only get someone to open this door. While we're fooling about and being gay, we've got to find out all we can about this castle."

Luckily, at that very moment the door opened, and the

giant Nurse bustled in saying, "Now, my poppets. Like to come and see the King and all the court setting out on the hunting? Such a pretty sight!"

They lost no time in rushing out past her and climbing down the first staircase they came to. The noise of hounds and horns and giant voices guided them, so that in a few minutes they reached the courtyard. The giants were all on foot, for there are no giant horses in that part of the world, and the giants' hunting is done on foot; like beagling in England. The hounds also were of normal size. When Jill saw that there were no horses she was at first dreadfully disappointed, for she felt sure that the great fat Queen would never go after hounds on foot; and it would never do to have her about the house all day. But then she saw the Queen in a kind of litter supported on the shoulders of six young giants. The silly old creature was all got up in green and had a horn at her side. Twenty or thirty giants, including the King, were assembled, ready for the sport, all talking and laughing fit to deafen you: and down below, nearer Jill's level, there were wagging tails, and barking, and loose, slobbery mouths and noses of dogs thrust into your hand. Puddleglum was just beginning to strike what he thought a gay and gamesome attitude (which might have spoiled everything if it had been noticed) when Jill put on her most attractively childish smile, rushed across to the Queen's litter and shouted up to the Queen.

"Oh, please! You're not going *away*, are you? You will come back?"

"Yes, my dear," said the Queen. "I'll be back tonight."

"Oh, *good*. How lovely!" said Jill. "And we *may* come to the feast tomorrow night, mayn't we? We're so longing for tomorrow night! And we do love being here. And while you're out, we may run over the whole castle and see everything, mayn't we? Do say yes."

The Queen did say yes, but the laughter of all the courtiers nearly drowned her voice.

Chapter Nine

How They Discovered Something Worth Knowing

THE OTHERS ADMITTED AFTERWARD THAT JILL HAD been wonderful that day. As soon as the King and the rest of the hunting party had set off, she began making a tour of the whole castle and asking questions, but all in such an innocent, babyish way that no one could suspect her of any secret design. Though her tongue was never still, you could hardly say she talked: she *prattled* and giggled. She made love to everyone—the grooms, the porters, the housemaids, the ladies-in-waiting, and the elderly giant lords whose hunting days were past. She submitted to being kissed and pawed about by any number of giant-esses, many of whom seemed sorry for her and called her "a poor little thing" though none of them explained why. She made especial friends with the cook and discovered the all-important fact there was a scullery door which let you out through the outer wall, so that you did not have to cross the courtyard or pass the great gatehouse. In the kitchen she pretended to be greedy, and ate all sorts of scraps which the cook and scullions delighted to give her. But upstairs among the ladies she asked questions about how she would be dressed for the great feast, and how long she would be allowed to sit up, and whether she would dance with some very, very small giant. And then (it made her hot all over when she remembered it afterward) she would put her head on one side in an idiotic fashion which grown-ups, giant and otherwise, thought very fetching, and shake her curls, and fidget, and say, "Oh, I do wish it was tomorrow night, don't you? Do you think the time will go quickly till then?" And all the giantesses said she was a perfect little darling; and some of them dabbed their eyes with enormous handkerchiefs as if they were going to cry.

"They're dear little things at that age," said one giantess to another. "It seems almost a pity . . ."

Scrubb and Puddleglum both did their best, but girls do that kind of thing better than boys. Even boys do it better than Marsh-wiggles.

At lunchtime something happened which made all three of them more anxious than ever to leave the castle of the Gentle Giants. They had lunch in the great hall at a little table of their own, near the fireplace. At a bigger table, about twenty yards away, half a dozen old giants were lunching. Their conversation was so noisy, and so high up in the air, that the children soon took no more notice of it than you would of hooters outside the window or traffic noises in the street. They were eating cold venison, a kind of food which Jill had never tasted before, and she was liking it.

Suddenly Puddleglum turned to them, and his face had gone so pale that you could see the paleness under the natural muddiness of his complexion. He said:

"Don't eat another bite."

"What's wrong?" asked the other two in a whisper.

"Didn't you hear what those giants were saying? 'That's a nice tender haunch of venison,' said one of them. 'Then that stag was a liar,' said another. 'Why?' said the first one. 'Oh,' said the other. 'They say that when he was caught he said, Don't kill me, I'm tough. You won't like me.'" For a moment Jill did not realize the full meaning of this. But she did when Scrubb's eyes opened wide with horror and he said:

"So we've been eating a *Talking* stag."

This discovery didn't have exactly the same effect on all of them. Jill, who was new to that world, was sorry for the poor stag and thought it rotten of the giants to have killed him. Scrubb, who had been in that world before and had at least one Talking beast as his dear friend, felt horrified; as you might feel about a murder. But Puddleglum, who was Narnian born, was sick and faint, and felt as you would feel if you found you had eaten a baby.

"We've brought the anger of Aslan on us," he said.

"That's what comes of not attending to the signs. We're under a curse, I expect. If it was allowed, it would be the best thing we could do, to take these knives and drive them into our own hearts."

And gradually even Jill came to see it from his point of view. At any rate, none of them wanted any more lunch. And as soon as they thought it safe they crept quietly out of the hall.

It was now drawing near to that time of the day on which their hopes of escape depended, and all became nervous. They hung about in passages and waited for things to become quiet. The giants in the hall sat on a dreadfully long time after the meal was over. The bald one was telling a story. When that was over, the three travelers dawdled down to the kitchen. But there were still plenty of giants there, or at least in the scullery, washing up and putting things away. It was agonizing, waiting till these finished their jobs and, one by one, wiped their hands and went away. At last only one old giantess was left in the room. She pottered about, and pottered about, and at last the three travelers realized with horror that she did not intend to go away at all.

"Well, dearies," she said to them. "That job's about through. Let's put the kettle there. That'll make a nice cup of tea presently. Now I can have a little bit of a rest. Just look into the scullery, like good poppets, and tell me if the back door is open."

"Yes, it is," said Scrubb.

"That's right. I always leave it open so as Puss can get in and out, the poor thing."

Then she sat down on one chair and put her feet up on another.

"I don't know as I mightn't have forty winks," said the giantess. "If only that blamey hunting party doesn't come back too soon."

All their spirits leaped up when she mentioned forty winks, and flopped down again when she mentioned the return of the hunting party.

"When do they usually come back?" asked Jill.

"You never can tell," said the giantess. "But there; go and be quiet for a bit, my dearies."

They retreated to the far end of the kitchen, and would have slipped out into the scullery there and then if the giantess had not sat up, opened her eyes, and brushed away a fly. "Don't try it till we're sure she's really asleep," whispered Scrubb. "Or it'll spoil everything." So they all huddled at the kitchen end, waiting and watching. The thought that the hunters might come back at any moment was terrible. And the giantess was fidgety. Whenever they thought she had really gone to sleep, she moved.

"I can't bear this," thought Jill. To distract her mind, she began looking about her. Just in front of her was a clean wide table with two clean pie-dishes on it, and an open book. They were giant pie-dishes of course. Jill thought that she could lie down just comfortably in one of them. Then she climbed up on the bench beside the table to look at the book. She read:

MALLARD. *This delicious bird can be cooked in a variety of ways.*

"It's a cookery book," thought Jill without much interest, and glanced over her shoulder. The giantess's eyes were shut but she didn't look as if she were properly asleep. Jill glanced back at the book. It was arranged alphabetically:

and at the very next entry her heart seemed to stop beating. It ran—

> MAN. *This elegant little biped has long been valued as a delicacy. It forms a traditional part of the Autumn Feast, and is served between the fish and the joint. Each Man—*

but she could not bear to read any more. She turned round. The giantess had waked up and was having a fit of coughing. Jill nudged the other two and pointed to the book. They also mounted the bench and bent over the huge pages. Scrubb was still reading about how to cook Men when Puddleglum pointed to the next entry below it. It was like this:

> MARSH-WIGGLE. *Some authorities reject this animal altogether as unfit for giants' consumption because of its stringy consistency and muddy flavor. The flavor can, however, be greatly reduced if—*

Jill touched his feet, and Scrubb's, gently. All three looked back at the giantess. Her mouth was slightly open and from her nose there came a sound which at that moment was more welcome to them than any music; she snored. And now it was a question of tip-toe work, not daring to go too fast, hardly daring to breathe, out through the scullery (giant sculleries smell horrid), out at last into the pale sunlight of a winter afternoon.

They were at the top of a rough little path which ran steeply down. And, thank heavens, on the right side of the castle; the City Ruinous was in sight. In a few minutes they were back on the broad, steep road which led down from the main gate of the castle. They were also in full view from every single window on that side. If it had been one, or two, or five windows there'd be a reasonable chance that no one might be looking out. But there were nearer fifty than five. They now realized, too, that the road on which they were, and indeed all the ground between them and the City Ruinous, didn't offer as much cover as would hide a fox: it was all coarse grass and pebbles and flat stones. To make matters worse, they were now in the clothes that the giants had provided for them last night: except Puddleglum, whom nothing would fit. Jill wore a vivid green robe, rather too long for her, and over that a scarlet mantle fringed with white fur. Scrubb had scarlet stockings, blue tunic and cloak, a gold-hilted sword, and a feathered bonnet.

"Nice bits of color, you two are," muttered Puddleglum. "Show up very prettily on a winter day. The worst archer in the world couldn't miss either of you if you were in range. And talking of archers, we'll be sorry not to have our own bows before long, I shouldn't wonder. Bit thin, too, those clothes of yours, are they?"

"Yes, I'm freezing already," said Jill.

A few minutes ago when they had been in the kitchen, she had thought that if only they could once get out of the castle, their escape would be almost complete. She now realized that the most dangerous part of it was still to come.

"Steady, steady," said Puddleglum. "Don't look back. Don't walk too quickly. Whatever you do, don't run. Look as if we were just taking a stroll, and then, if anyone sees us, he might, just possibly, not bother. The moment we look like people running away, we're done."

The distance to the City Ruinous seemed longer than Jill would have believed possible. But bit by bit they were covering it. Then came a noise. The other two gasped. Jill, who didn't know what it was, said, "What's that?"

"Hunting horn," whispered Scrubb.

"But don't run even now," said Puddleglum. "Not till I give the word."

This time Jill couldn't help glancing over her shoulder. There, about half a mile away, was the hunt returning from behind them on the left.

They walked on. Suddenly a great clamor of giant voices arose: then shouts and hollas.

"They've seen us. Run," said Puddleglum.

Jill gathered up her long skirts—horrible things for running in—and ran. There was no mistaking the danger now. She could hear the music of the hounds. She could hear the King's voice roaring out, "After them, after them, or we'll have no man-pies tomorrow."

She was last of the three now, cumbered with her dress, slipping on loose stones, her hair getting in her mouth, running-pains across her chest. The hounds were much nearer. Now she had to run uphill, up the stony slope which led to the lowest step of the giant stairway. She had no idea what they would do when they got there, or how they would be any better off even if they reached the top. But she didn't think about that. She was like a hunted animal now; as long as the pack was after her, she must run till she dropped.

The Marsh-wiggle was ahead. As he came to the lowest step he stopped, looked a little to his right, and all of a sudden darted into a little hole or crevice at the bottom of it. His long legs, disappearing into it, looked very like those of a spider. Scrubb hesitated and then vanished after him. Jill, breathless and reeling, came to the place about a minute later. It was an unattractive hole—a crack between the earth and the stone about three feet long and hardly more than a foot high. You had to fling yourself flat on your face and crawl in. You couldn't do it so very quickly either. She felt sure that a dog's teeth would close on her heel before she got inside.

"Quick, quick. Stones. Fill up the opening," came Puddleglum's voice in the darkness beside her. It was pitch black in there, except for the gray light in the opening by which they had crawled in. The other two were working

hard. She could see Scrubb's small hands and the Marsh-
wiggle's big, frog-like hands black against the light, working desperately to pile up stones. Then she realized how
important this was and began groping for large stones herself, and handing them to the others. Before the dogs were
baying and yelping at the cave mouth, they had it pretty
well filled; and now, of course, there was no light at all.

"Farther in, quick," said Puddleglum's voice.

"Let's all hold hands," said Jill.

"Good idea," said Scrubb. But it took them quite a long
time to find one another's hands in the darkness. The dogs
were sniffing at the other side of the barrier now.

"Try if we can stand up," suggested Scrubb. They did
and found that they could. Then, Puddleglum holding
out a hand behind him to Scrubb, and Scrubb holding a
hand out behind him to Jill (who wished very much that
she was the middle one of the party and not the last), they
began groping with their feet and stumbling forward into
the blackness. It was all loose stones underfoot. Then
Puddleglum came up to a wall of rock. They turned a little
to their right and went on. There were a good many more

twists and turns. Jill had now no sense of direction at all, and no idea where the mouth of the cave lay.

"The question is," came Puddleglum's voice out of the darkness ahead, "whether, taking one thing with another, it wouldn't be better to go back (if we *can*) and give the giants a treat at that feast of theirs, instead of losing our way in the guts of a hill where, ten to one, there's dragons and deep holes and gases and water and— Ow! Let go! Save yourselves. I'm—"

After that all happened quickly. There was a wild cry, a swishing, dusty, gravelly noise, a rattle of stones, and Jill found herself sliding, sliding, hopelessly sliding, and sliding quicker every moment down a slope that grew steeper every moment. It was not a smooth, firm slope, but a slope of small stones and rubbish. Even if you could have stood up, it would have been no use. Any bit of that slope you had put your foot on would have slid away from under you and carried you down with it. But Jill was more lying than standing. And the farther they all slid, the more they disturbed all the stones and earth, so that the general downward rush of everything (including themselves) got faster and louder and dustier and dirtier. From the sharp cries and swearing of the other two, Jill got the idea that many of the stones she was dislodging were hitting Scrubb and Puddleglum pretty hard. And now she was going at a furious rate and felt sure she would be broken to bits at the bottom.

Yet somehow they weren't. They were a mass of bruises, and the wet, sticky stuff on her face appeared to be blood. And such a mass of loose earth, shingle, and larger stones was piled up round her (and partly over her) that she couldn't get up. The darkness was so complete that it made no difference at all whether you had your eyes open or shut. There was no noise. And that was the very worst moment Jill had ever known in her life. Supposing she was alone: supposing the others... Then she heard movements around her. And presently all three, in shaken voices, were explaining that none of them seemed to have any broken bones.

"We can never get up that again," said Scrubb's voice.

"And have you noticed how warm it is?" said the voice of Puddleglum. "That means we're a long way down.

Might be nearly a mile."

No one said anything. Some time later Puddleglum added:

"My tinder-box has gone."

After another long pause Jill said, "I'm terribly thirsty."

No one suggested doing anything. There was so obviously nothing to be done. For the moment, they did not feel it quite so badly as one might have expected; that was because they were so tired.

Long, long afterward, without the slightest warning, an utterly strange voice spoke. They knew at once that it was not the one voice in the whole world for which each had secretly been hoping; the voice of Aslan. It was a dark, flat voice—almost, if you know what that means, a pitch-black voice. It said:

"What make you here, creatures of the Overworld?"

Chapter Ten

Travels Without the Sun

"WHO'S THERE?" SHOUTED THE THREE TRAVELERS.

"I am the Warden of the Marches of Underland, and with me stand a hundred Earthmen in arms," came the reply. "Tell me quickly who you are and what is your errand in the Deep Realm?"

"We fell down by accident," said Puddleglum, truthfully enough.

"Many fall down, and few return to the sunlit lands,"

said the voice. "Make ready now to come with me to the Queen of the Deep Realm."

"What does she want with us?" asked Scrubb cautiously.

"I do not know," said the voice. "Her will is not to be questioned but obeyed."

While he said these words there was a noise like a soft explosion and immediately a cold light, gray with a little blue in it, flooded the cavern. All hope that the speaker had been idly boasting when he spoke of his hundred armed followers died at once. Jill found herself blinking and staring at a dense crowd. They were of all sizes, from little gnomes barely a foot high to stately figures taller than men. All carried three-pronged spears in their hands, and all were dreadfully pale, and all stood as still as statues. Apart from that, they were very different; some had tails and others not, some wore great beards and others had very round, smooth faces, big as pumpkins. There were long, pointed noses, and long, soft noses like small trunks, and great blobby noses. Several had single horns in the middle of their foreheads. But in one respect they were all alike: every face in the whole hundred was as sad as a face could be. They were so sad that, after the first glance, Jill almost forgot to be afraid of them. She felt she would like to cheer them up.

"Well!" said Puddleglum, rubbing his hands. "This is just what I needed. If these chaps don't teach me to take a serious view of life, I don't know what will. Look at that fellow with the walrus mustache—or that one with the—"

"Get up," said the leader of the Earthmen.

There was nothing else to be done. The three travelers scrambled to their feet and joined hands. One wanted the touch of a friend's hand at a moment like that. And the Earthmen came all round them, padding on large, soft feet, on which some had ten toes, some twelve, and others none.

"March," said the Warden: and march they did.

The cold light came from a large ball on top of a long pole, and the tallest of the gnomes carried this at the head of the procession. By its cheerless rays they could see that they were in a natural cavern; the walls and roof were knobbed, twisted, and gashed into a thousand fantastic shapes, and the stony floor sloped downward as they proceeded. It was worse for Jill than the others, because she hated dark, underground places. And when, as they went on, the cave got lower and narrower, and when, at last, the light-bearer stood aside, and the gnomes, one by one, stooped down (all except the very smallest ones) and stepped into a little dark crack and disappeared, she felt she could bear it no longer.

"I can't go in there, I can't! I can't! I won't!" she panted. The Earthmen said nothing but they all lowered their spears and pointed them at her.

"Steady, Pole," said Puddleglum. "Those big fellows wouldn't be crawling in there if it didn't get wider later on. And there's one thing about this underground work, we shan't get any rain."

"Oh, you don't understand. I can't," wailed Jill.

"Think how *I* felt on that cliff, Pole," said Scrubb. "You go first, Puddleglum, and I'll come after her."

"That's right," said the Marsh-wiggle, getting down on his hands and knees. "You keep a grip of my heels, Pole, and Scrubb will hold on to yours. Then we'll all be comfortable."

"Comfortable!" said Jill. But she got down and they

crawled in on their elbows. It was a nasty place. You had to go flat on your face for what seemed like half an hour, though it may really have been only five minutes. It was hot. Jill felt she was being smothered. But at last a dim light showed ahead, the tunnel grew wider and higher, and they came out, hot, dirty, and shaken, into a cave so large that it scarcely seemed a cave at all.

It was full of a dim, drowsy radiance, so that here they had no need of the Earthmen's strange lantern. The floor was soft with some kind of moss and out of this grew many strange shapes, branched and tall like trees, but flabby like mushrooms. They stood too far apart to make a forest; it was more like a park. The light (a greenish gray) seemed to come both from them and from the moss, and it was not strong enough to reach the roof of the cave, which must have been a long way overhead. Across the mild, soft, sleepy place they were now made to march. It was very sad, but with a quiet sort of sadness, like soft music.

Here they passed dozens of strange animals lying on the turf, either dead or asleep, Jill could not tell which. These were mostly of a dragonish or bat-like sort; Puddleglum did not know what any of them were.

"Do they grow here?" Scrubb asked the Warden. He seemed very surprised at being spoken to, but replied, "No. They are all beasts that have found their way down by chasms and caves, out of Overland into the Deep Realm. Many come down, and few return to the sunlit lands. It is said that they will all wake at the end of the world."

His mouth shut like a box when he had said this, and in the great silence of that cave the children felt that they would not dare to speak again. The bare feet of the gnomes, padding on the deep moss, made no sound. There was no wind, there were no birds, there was no sound of water. There was no sound of breathing from the strange beasts.

When they had walked for several miles, they came to a wall of rock, and in it a low archway leading into another cavern. It was not, however, so bad as the last entrance and Jill could go through it without bending her head. It brought them into a smaller cave, long and narrow, about the shape and size of a cathedral. And here, filling almost the whole length of it, lay an enormous man fast asleep. He was far bigger than any of the giants, and his face was not like a giant's, but noble and beautiful. His breast rose and fell gently under the snowy beard which covered him to the waist. A pure, silver light (no one saw where it came from) rested upon him.

"Who's that?" asked Puddleglum. And it was so long since anyone had spoken, that Jill wondered how he had the nerve.

"That is old Father Time, who was once a King in Overland," said the Warden. "And now he has sunk down into the Deep Realm and lies dreaming of all the things that are done in the upper world. Many sink down, and few return to the sunlit lands. They say he will wake at the end of the world."

And out of that cave they passed into another, and then into another and another, and so on till Jill lost count, but always they were going downhill and each cave was lower than the last, till the very thought of the weight and depth of the earth above you was suffocating. At last they came to a place where the Warden commanded his cheerless lantern to be lit again. Then they passed into a cave so wide and dark that they could see nothing of it except that right in front of them a strip of pale sand ran down into still water. And there, beside a little jetty, lay a ship without mast or sail but with many oars. They were made to go on board her and led forward to the bows where there was a clear space in front of the rowers' benches and a seat running round inside the bulwarks.

"One thing I'd like to know," said Puddleglum, "is whether anyone from our world—from up-a-top, I mean—has ever done this trip before?"

"Many have taken ship at the pale beaches," replied the Warden, "and—"

"Yes, I know," interrupted Puddleglum. "*And few return to the sunlit lands.* You needn't say it again. You *are* a chap of one idea, aren't you?"

The children huddled close together on each side of Puddleglum. They had thought him a wet blanket while they were still above ground, but down here he seemed the only comforting thing they had. Then the pale lantern was hung up amidships, the Earthmen sat to the oars, and the ship began to move. The lantern cast its light only a very short way. Looking ahead, they could see nothing but smooth, dark water, fading into absolute blackness.

"Oh, whatever will become of us?" said Jill despairingly.

"Now, don't you let your spirits down, Pole," said the Marsh-wiggle. "There's one thing you've got to remember. We're back on the right lines. We were to go under the Ruined City, and we *are* under it. We're following the instructions again."

Presently they were given food—flat, flabby cakes of some sort which had hardly any taste. And after that, they gradually fell asleep. But when they woke, everything was just the same; the gnomes still rowing, the ship still gliding on, still dead blackness ahead. How often they woke and slept and ate and slept again, none of them could ever remember. And the worst thing about it was that you began to feel as if you had always lived on that ship, in that darkness, and to wonder whether sun and blue skies and wind and birds had not been only a dream.

They had almost given up hoping or being afraid about anything when at last they saw lights ahead: dreary lights, like that of their own lantern. Then, quite suddenly, one of these lights came close and they saw that they were passing another ship. After that they met several ships. Then, staring till their eyes hurt, they saw that some of the lights ahead were shining on what looked like wharfs, walls, towers, and moving crowds. But still there was hardly any noise.

"By Jove," said Scrubb. "A city!" and soon they all saw that he was right.

But it was a queer city. The lights were so few and far apart that they would hardly have done for scattered cottages in our world. But the little bits of the place which you could see by the lights were like glimpses of a great seaport. You could make out in one place a whole crowd of ships loading or unloading; in another, bales of stuff and warehouses; in a third, walls and pillars that suggested great palaces or temples; and always, wherever the light fell, endless crowds—hundreds of Earthmen, jostling one another as they padded softly about their business in narrow streets, broad squares, or up great flights of steps. Their continued movement made a sort of soft, murmuring noise as the ship drew nearer and nearer; but there was not a song or a shout or a bell or the rattle of a wheel anywhere.

The City was as quiet, and nearly as dark, as the inside of an ant-hill.

At last their ship was brought alongside a quay and made fast. The three travelers were taken ashore and marched up into the City. Crowds of Earthmen, no two alike, rubbed shoulders with them in the crowded streets, and the sad light fell on many sad and grotesque faces. But no one showed any interest in the strangers. Every gnome seemed to be as busy as it was sad, though Jill never found what they were so busy about. But the endless moving, shoving, hurrying, and the soft pad-pad-pad went on.

At last they came to what appeared to be a great castle, though few of the windows in it were lighted. Here they were taken in and made to cross a courtyard, and to climb many staircases. This brought them in the end to a great murkily lit hall. But in one corner of it—oh joy!—there was an archway filled with a quite different sort of light; the honest, yellowish, warm light of such a lamp as humans use. What showed by this light inside the archway was the foot of a staircase which wound upward between walls of stone. The light seemed to come from the top. Two Earthmen stood one on each side of the arch like sentries, or footmen.

The Warden went up to these two, and said, as if it were a password:

"Many sink down to the Underworld."

"And few return to the sunlit lands," they answered, as if it were the countersign. Then all three put their heads together and talked. At last one of the two gnomes-in-waiting said, "I tell you the Queen's grace is gone from hence on her great affair. We had best keep these top dwellers in strait prison till her homecoming. Few return to the sunlit lands."

At that moment the conversation was interrupted by what seemed to Jill the most delightful noise in the world. It came from above, from the top of the staircase; and it was a clear, ringing, perfectly human voice, the voice of a young man.

"What coil are you keeping down there, Mulluguth-erum?" it shouted. "Overworlders, ha! Bring them up to me, and that presently."

"Please it your Highness to remember," began

Mullugutherum, but the voice cut him short.

"It pleases my Highness principally to be obeyed, old mutterer. Bring them up," it called.

Mullugutherum shook his head, motioned to the travelers to follow and began going up the staircase. At every step the light increased. There were rich tapestries hanging on the walls. The lamplight shone golden through thin curtains at the staircase-head. The Earthmen parted the curtains and stood aside. The three passed in. They were in a beautiful room, richly tapestried, with a bright fire on a clean hearth, and red wine and cut glass sparkling on the table. A young man with fair hair rose to greet them. He was handsome and looked both bold and kind, though there was something about his face that didn't seem quite right. He was dressed in black and altogether looked a little bit like Hamlet.

"Welcome, Overworlders," he cried. "But stay a moment! I cry you mercy! I have seen you two fair children, and this, your strange governor, before. Was it not you three that met me by the bridge on the borders of Ettinsmoor when I rode there by my Lady's side?"

"Oh . . . you were the black knight who never spoke?" exclaimed Jill.

"And was that lady the Queen of Underland?" asked Puddleglum, in no very friendly voice. And Scrubb, who was thinking the same, burst out, "Because if it was, I think she was jolly mean to send us off to a castle of giants who intended to eat us. What harm had we ever done her, I should like to know?"

"How?" said the Black Knight with a frown. "If you were not so young a warrior, Boy, you and I must have fought to the death on this quarrel. I can hear no words against my Lady's honor. But of this you may be assured, that whatever she said to you, she said of a good intent. You do not know her. She is a nosegay of all virtues, as truth, mercy, constancy, gentleness, courage, and the rest. I say what I know. Her kindness to me alone, who can in no way reward her, would make an admirable history. But you shall know and love her hereafter. Meanwhile, what is your errand in the Deep Lands?"

And before Puddleglum could stop her, Jill blurted out, "Please, we are trying to find Prince Rilian of Narnia."

And then she realized what a frightful risk she had taken; these people might be enemies. But the Knight showed no interest.

"Rilian? Narnia?" he said carelessly. "Narnia? What land is that? I have never heard the name. It must be a thousand leagues from those parts of the Overworld that I know. But it was a strange fantasy that brought you seeking this—how do you call him?—Billian? Trillian? in my Lady's realm. Indeed, to my certain knowledge, there is no such man here." He laughed very loudly at this, and Jill thought to herself, "I wonder is *that* what's wrong with his face? Is he a bit silly?"

"We had been told to look for a message on the stones of the City Ruinous," said Scrubb. "And we saw the words UNDER ME."

The Knight laughed even more heartily than before. "You were the more deceived," he said. "Those words meant nothing to your purpose. Had you but asked my Lady, she could have given you better counsel. For those words are all that is left of a longer script, which in ancient times, as she well remembers, expressed this verse:

Though under Earth and throneless now I be,
Yet, while I lived, all Earth was under me.

"From which it is plain that some great king of the ancient giants, who lies buried there, caused this boast to be cut in the stone over his sepulcher; though the breaking up of some stones, and the carrying away of others for new buildings, and the filling up of the cuts with rubble, has left only two words that can still be read. Is it not the merriest jest in the world that you should have thought they were written to you?"

This was like cold water down the back to Scrubb and Jill; for it seemed to them very likely that the words had nothing to do with their quest at all, and that they had been taken in by a mere accident.

"Don't you mind him," said Puddleglum. "There *are* no accidents. Our guide is Aslan; and he was there when the giant King caused the letters to be cut, and he knew already all things that would come of them, including *this*."

"This guide of yours must be a long liver, friend," said the Knight with another of his laughs.

Jill began to find them a little irritating.

"And it seems to me, Sir," answered Puddleglum, "that this Lady of yours must be a long liver too, if she remembers the verse as it was when they first cut it."

"Very shrewd, Frog-face," said the Knight, clapping Puddleglum on the shoulder and laughing again. "And you have hit the truth. She is of divine race, and knows neither age nor death. I am the more thankful to her for all her infinite bounty to such a poor mortal wretch as I. For you must know, Sirs, I am a man under most strange afflictions, and none but the Queen's grace would have had patience with me. Patience, said I? But it goes far beyond that. She has promised me a great kingdom in Overland and, when I am king, her own most gracious hand in marriage. But the tale is too long for you to hear fasting and standing. Hi there, some of you! Bring wine and Updwellers' food for my guests. Please you, be seated, gentlemen. Little maiden, sit in this chair. You shall hear it all."

Chapter Eleven

In the Dark Castle

WHEN THE MEAL (WHICH WAS PIGEON PIE, COLD ham, salad, and cakes) had been brought, and all had drawn their chairs up to the table and begun, the Knight continued:

"You must understand, friends, that I know nothing of who I was and whence I came into this Dark World. I remember no time when I was not dwelling, as now, at the court of this all but heavenly Queen; but my thought is that she saved me from some evil enchantment and brought me hither of her exceeding bounty. (Honest Frog-foot, your cup is empty. Suffer me to refill it.) And this seems to me the likelier because even now I am bound by a spell, from which my Lady alone can free me. Every night there comes an hour when my mind is most horribly changed and, after my mind, my body. For first I become furious and wild and would rush upon my dearest friends to kill them, if I were not bound. And soon after that, I turn into the likeness of a great serpent, hungry, fierce, and deadly. (Sir, be pleased to take another breast of pigeon, I entreat you.) So they tell me, and they certainly speak truth, for my Lady says the same. I myself know nothing of it, for when my hour is past I awake forgetful of all that vile fit and in my proper shape and sound mind—saving that I am somewhat wearied. (Little lady, eat one of these honey cakes, which are brought for me from some barbarous land in the far south of the world.) Now the Queen's majesty knows by her art that I shall be freed from this enchantment when once she has made me king of a land in the Overworld and set its crown upon my head. The land is already chosen and the very place of our breaking out. Her

Earthmen have worked day and night digging a way beneath it, and have now gone so far and so high that they tunnel not a score of feet beneath the very grass on which the Updwellers of that country walk. It will be very soon now that those Uplanders' fate will come upon them. She herself is at the diggings tonight, and I expect a message to go to her. Then the thin roof of earth which still keeps me from my kingdom will be broken through, and with her to guide me and a thousand Earthmen at my back, I shall ride forth in arms, fall suddenly on our enemies, slay their chief man, cast down their strong places, and doubtless be their crowned king within four and twenty hours."

"It's a bit rough luck on *them*, isn't it?" said Scrubb.

"Thou art a lad of a wondrous, quick-working wit!" exclaimed the Knight. "For, on my honor, I had never thought of it so before. I see your meaning." He looked slightly, very slightly troubled for a moment or two; but his face soon cleared and he broke out, with another of his loud laughs, "But fie on gravity! Is it not the most comical and ridiculous thing in the world to think of them all going about their business and never dreaming that under their peaceful fields and floors, only a fathom down, there is a great army ready to break out upon them like a fountain! And they never to have suspected! Why, they themselves, when once the first smart of their defeat is over, can hardly choose but laugh at the thought!"

"I don't think it's funny at all," said Jill. "I think you'll be a wicked tyrant."

"What?" said the Knight, still laughing and patting her head in a quite infuriating fashion. "Is our little maid a deep politician? But never fear, sweetheart. In ruling that land, I shall do all by the counsel of my Lady, who will then be my Queen too. Her word shall be my law, even as my word will be law to the people we have conquered."

"Where I come from," said Jill, who was disliking him more every minute, "they don't think much of men who are bossed about by their wives."

"Shalt think otherwise when thou hast a man of thine own, I warrant you," said the Knight, apparently thinking this very funny. "But with my Lady, it is another matter. I am well content to live by her word, who has already saved me from a thousand dangers. No mother has taken pains more tenderly for her child, than the Queen's grace has for me. Why, look you, amid all her cares and business, she rideth out with me in the Overworld many a time and oft to accustom my eyes to the sunlight. And then I must go fully armed and with visor down, so that no man may see my face, and I must speak to no one. For she has found out by art magical that this would hinder my deliverance from the grievous enchantment I lie under. Is not that a lady worthy of a man's whole worship?"

"Sounds a very nice lady indeed," said Puddleglum in a voice which meant exactly the opposite.

They were thoroughly tired of the Knight's talk before they had finished supper. Puddleglum was thinking, "I wonder what game that witch is really playing with this young fool." Scrubb was thinking, "He's a great baby, really: tied to that woman's apron strings; he's a sap." And Jill was thinking, "He's the silliest, most conceited, selfish pig I've met for a long time." But when the meal was over, the Knight's mood had changed. There was no more laughter about him.

"Friends," he said, "my hour is now very near. I am

ashamed that you should see me yet I dread being left alone. They will come in presently and bind me hand and foot to yonder chair. Alas, so it must be: for in my fury, they tell me, I would destroy all that I could reach."

"I say," said Scrubb, "I'm awfully sorry about your enchantment of course, but what will those fellows do to *us* when they come to bind you? They talked of putting us in prison. And we don't like all those dark places very much. We'd much rather stay here till you're ... better ... if we may."

"It is well thought of," said the Knight. "By custom none but the Queen herself remains with me in my evil hour. Such is her tender care for my honor that she would not willingly suffer any ears but her own to hear the words I utter in that frenzy. But I could not easily persuade my attendant gnomes that you should be left with me. And I think I hear their soft feet even now upon the stairs. Go through yonder door: it leads into my other apartments. And there, either await my coming when they have unbound me; or, if you will, return and sit with me in my ravings."

They followed his directions and passed out of the room by a door which they had not yet seen opened. It brought them, they were pleased to see, not into darkness but into a lighted corridor. They tried various doors and found (what they very badly needed) water for washing and even a looking glass. "He never offered us a wash before supper," said Jill, drying her face. "Selfish, self-centered pig."

"Are we going back to watch the enchantment, or shall we stay here?" said Scrubb.

"Stay here, I vote," said Jill. "I'd much rather not see it." But she felt a little inquisitive all the same.

"No, go back," said Puddleglum. "We may pick up some information, and we need all we can get. I am sure that Queen is a witch and an enemy. And those Earthmen would knock us on the head as soon as look at us. There's a stronger smell of danger and lies and magic and treason about this land than I've ever smelled before. We need to keep our eyes and ears open."

They went back down the corridor and gently pushed the door open. "It's all right," said Scrubb, meaning that there were no Earthmen about. Then they all came back into the room where they had supped.

The main door was now shut, concealing the curtain between which they had first entered. The Knight was seated in a curious silver chair, to which he was bound by his ankles, his knees, his elbows, his wrists, and his waist. There was sweat on his forehead and his face was filled with anguish.

"Come in, friends," he said, glancing quickly up. "The fit is not yet upon me. Make no noise, for I told that prying chamberlain that you were in bed. Now . . . I can feel it coming. Quick! Listen while I am master of myself. When the fit is upon me, it well may be that I shall beg and implore you, with entreaties and threatenings, to loosen my bonds. They say I do. I shall call upon you by all that is most dear and most dreadful. But do not listen to me. Harden your hearts and stop your ears. For while I am bound you are safe. But if once I were up and out of this chair, then first would come my fury, and after that"—he shuddered—"the change into a loathsome serpent."

"There's no fear of our loosing you," said Puddleglum. "We've no wish to meet wild men; or serpents either."

"I should think not," said Scrubb and Jill together.

"All the same," added Puddleglum in a whisper. "Don't let's be too sure. Let's be on our guard. We've muffed everything else, you know. He'll be cunning, I shouldn't wonder, once he gets started. Can we trust one another? Do we all promise that whatever he says we don't touch those cords? *Whatever* he says, mind you?"

"Rather!" said Scrubb.

"There's nothing in the world he can say or do that'll make me change my mind," said Jill.

"Hush! Something's happening," said Puddleglum.

The Knight was moaning. His face was as pale as putty, and he writhed in his bonds. And whether because she was sorry for him, or for some other reason, Jill thought that he looked a nicer sort of man than he had looked before.

"Ah," he groaned. "Enchantments, enchantments . . . the heavy, tangled, cold, clammy web of evil magic. Buried alive. Dragged down under the earth, down into the sooty blackness . . . how many years is it? . . . Have I lived ten years, or a thousand years, in the pit? Maggotmen all around me. Oh, have mercy. Let me out, let me go back. Let me feel the wind and see the sky . . . There used to be a little pool. When you looked down into it you could see all the trees growing upside-down in the water, all green, and below them, deep, very deep, the blue sky."

He had been speaking in a low voice; now he looked up, fixed his eyes upon them, and said loud and clear:

"Quick! I am sane now. Every night I am sane. If only I could get out of this enchanted chair, it would last. I should be a man again. But every night they bind me, and so every night my chance is gone. But you are not enemies. I am not *your* prisoner. Quick! Cut these cords."

"Stand fast! Steady," said Puddleglum to the two children.

"I beseech you to hear me," said the Knight, forcing himself to speak calmly. "Have they told you that if I am released from this chair I shall kill you and become a serpent? I see by your faces that they have. It is a lie. It is at this hour that I am in my right mind: it is all the rest of the day that I am enchanted. You are not Earthmen nor witches. Why should you be on their side? Of your courtesy, cut my bonds."

"Steady! Steady! Steady!" said the three travelers to one another.

"Oh, you have hearts of stone," said the Knight. "Believe me, you look upon a wretch who has suffered almost more than any mortal heart can bear. What wrong have I ever done you, that you should side with my enemies to keep me in such miseries? And the minutes are slipping past. *Now* you can save me; when this hour has passed, I shall be witless again—the toy and lap-dog, nay, more likely the pawn and tool, of the most devilish sorceress that ever planned the woe of men. And this night, of all nights, when she is away! You take from me a chance that may never come again."

"This is dreadful. I do wish we'd stayed away till it was over," said Jill.

"Steady!" said Puddleglum.

The prisoner's voice was now rising into a shriek. "Let me go, I say. Give me my sword. My sword! Once I am free, I shall take such revenge on Earthmen that Underland will talk of it for a thousand years!"

"Now the frenzy is beginning," said Scrubb. "I hope those knots are all right."

"Yes," said Puddleglum. "He'd have twice his natural strength if he got free now. And I'm not clever with my sword. He'd get us both, I shouldn't wonder; and then Pole on her own would be left to tackle the snake."

The prisoner was now so straining at his bonds that they cut into his wrists and ankles. "Beware," he said. "Beware. One night I *did* break them. But the witch was there that time. You will not have her to help you tonight. Free me now, and I am your friend. I'm your mortal enemy else."

"Cunning, isn't he?" said Puddleglum.

"Once and for all," said the prisoner, "I adjure you to set me free. By all fears and all loves, by the bright skies of Overland, by the great Lion, by Aslan himself, I charge you—"

"Oh!" cried the three travelers as though they had been hurt. "It's the sign," said Puddleglum. "It was the *words* of the sign," said Scrubb more cautiously. "Oh, what *are* we to do?" said Jill.

It was a dreadful question. What had been the use of promising one another that they would not on any account set the Knight free, if they were now to do so the first time he happened to call upon a name they really cared about? On the other hand, what had been the use of learning the signs if they weren't going to obey them? Yet could Aslan have really meant them to unbind anyone— even a lunatic—who asked it in his name? Could it be a mere accident? Or how if the Queen of the Underworld knew all about the signs and had made the Knight learn this name simply in order to entrap them? But then, supposing this was the real sign? . . . They had muffed three already; they daren't muff the fourth.

"Oh, if only we knew!" said Jill.

"I think we do know," said Puddleglum.

"Do you mean you think everything will come right if we do untie him?" said Scrubb.

"I don't know about that," said Puddleglum. "You see, Aslan didn't tell Pole what would happen. He only told her what to do. That fellow will be the death of us once he's up, I shouldn't wonder. But that doesn't let us off following the sign."

They all stood looking at one another with bright eyes.

It was a sickening moment. "All right!" said Jill suddenly. "Let's get it over. Good-bye, everyone!..." They all shook hands. The Knight was screaming by now; there was foam on his cheeks.

"Come on, Scrubb," said Puddleglum. He and Scrubb drew their swords and went over to the captive.

"In the name of Aslan," they said and began methodically cutting the cords. The instant the prisoner was free, he crossed the room in a single bound, seized his own sword (which had been taken from him and laid on the table), and drew it.

"You first!" he cried and fell upon the silver chair. That must have been a good sword. The silver gave way before its edge like string, and in a moment a few twisted fragments, shining on the floor, were all that was left. But as the chair broke, there came from it a bright flash, a sound like small thunder, and (for one moment) a loathsome smell.

"Lie there, vile engine of sorcery," he said, "lest your mistress should ever use you for another victim." Then he turned and surveyed his rescuers; and the something wrong, whatever it was, had vanished from his face.

"What?" he cried, turning to Puddleglum. "Do I see before me a Marsh-wiggle—a real, live, honest, Narnian Marsh-wiggle?"

"Oh, so you *have* heard of Narnia after all?" said Jill.

"Had I forgotten it when I was under the spell?" asked the Knight. "Well, that and all other bedevilments are now over. You may well believe that I know Narnia, for I am Rilian, Prince of Narnia, and Caspian the great King is my father."

"Your Royal Highness," said Puddleglum, sinking on one knee (and the children did the same), "we have come hither for no other end than to seek you."

"And who are you, my other deliverers?" said the Prince to Scrubb and Jill.

"We were sent by Aslan himself from beyond the world's end to seek your Highness," said Scrubb. "I am Eustace who sailed with him to the island of Ramandu."

"I owe all three of you a greater debt than I can ever pay," said Prince Rilian. "But my father? Is he yet alive?"

"He sailed east again before we left Narnia, my lord," said Puddleglum. "But your Highness must consider that the King is very old. It is ten to one his Majesty must die on the voyage."

"He is old, you say. How long then have I been in the power of the witch?"

"It is more than ten years since your Highness was lost in the woods at the north side of Narnia."

"Ten years!" said the Prince, drawing his hand across his face as if to rub away the past. "Yes, I believe you. For now that I am myself I can remember that enchanted life, though while I was enchanted I could not remember my true self. And now, fair friends—but wait! I hear their feet (does it not sicken a man, that padding woolly tread! faugh!) on the stairs. Lock the door, boy. Or stay. I have a better thought than that. I will fool these Earthmen, if Aslan gives me the wit. Take your cue from me."

He walked resolutely to the door and flung it wide open.

Chapter Twelve

The Queen of Underland

TWO EARTHMEN ENTERED, BUT INSTEAD OF advancing into the room, they placed themselves one on each side of the door, and bowed deeply. They were followed immediately by the last person whom anyone had expected or wished to see: the Lady of the Green Kirtle, the Queen of Underland. She stood dead still in the doorway, and they could see her eyes moving as she took in the whole situation—the three strangers, the silver chair destroyed, and the Prince free, with his sword in his hand.

She turned very white; but Jill thought it was the sort of whiteness that comes over some people's faces not when they are frightened but when they are angry. For a moment the Witch fixed her eyes on the Prince, and there was murder in them. Then she seemed to change her mind.

"Leave us," she said to the two Earthmen. "And let none disturb us till I call, on pain of death." The gnomes padded away obediently, and the Witch-queen shut and locked the door.

"How now, my lord Prince," she said. "Has your nightly fit not yet come upon you, or is it over so soon? Why stand you here unbound? Who are these aliens? And is it they who have destroyed the chair which was your only safety?"

Prince Rilian shivered as she spoke to him. And no wonder: it is not easy to throw off in half an hour an enchantment which has made one a slave for ten years. Then, speaking with a great effort, he said:

"Madam, there will be no more need of that chair. And you, who have told me a hundred times how deeply you pitied me for the sorceries by which I was bound, will doubtless hear with joy that they are now ended forever. There was, it seems, some small error in your Ladyship's way of treating them. These, my true friends, have delivered me. I am now in my right mind, and there are two things I will say to you. First—as for your Ladyship's design of putting me at the head of an army of Earthmen so that I may break out into the Overworld and there, by main force, make myself king over some nation that never did me wrong—murdering their natural lords and holding their throne as a bloody and foreign tyrant—now that I know myself, I do utterly abhor and renounce it as plain villainy. And second: I am the King's son of Narnia, Rilian, the only child of Caspian, Tenth of that name, whom some call Caspian the Seafarer. Therefore, Madam, it is my purpose, as it is also my duty, to depart suddenly from your Highness's court into my own country. Please it you to grant me and my friends safe conduct and a guide through your dark realm."

Now the Witch said nothing at all, but moved gently across the room, always keeping her face and eyes very

steadily toward the Prince. When she had come to a little
ark set in the wall not far from the fireplace, she opened it,
and took out first a handful of a green powder. This she
threw on the fire. It did not blaze much, but a very sweet
and drowsy smell came from it. And all through the conversation which followed, that smell grew stronger, and
filled the room, and made it harder to think. Secondly, she
took out a musical instrument rather like a mandolin. She
began to play it with her fingers—a steady, monotonous
thrumming that you didn't notice after a few minutes. But
the less you noticed it, the more it got into your brain and
your blood. This also made it hard to think. After she had
thrummed for a time (and the sweet smell was now strong)
she began speaking in a sweet, quiet voice.

"Narnia?" she said. "Narnia? I have often heard your
Lordship utter that name in your ravings. Dear Prince,
you are very sick. There is no land called Narnia."

"Yes there is, though, Ma'am," said Puddleglum. "You
see, I happen to have lived there all my life."

"Indeed," said the Witch. "Tell me, I pray you, where
that country is?"

"Up there," said Puddleglum, stoutly, pointing over-head. "I—I don't know exactly where."

"How?" said the Queen, with a kind, soft, musical laugh. "Is there a country up among the stones and mortar on the roof?"

"No," said Puddleglum, struggling a little to get his breath. "It's in Overworld."

"And what, or where, pray is this . . . how do you call it . . . *Overworld?*"

"Oh, don't be so silly," said Scrubb, who was fighting hard against the enchantment of the sweet smell and the thrumming. "As if you didn't know! It's up above, up where you can see the sky and the sun and the stars. Why, you've been there yourself. We met you there."

"I cry you mercy, little brother," laughed the Witch (you couldn't have heard a lovelier laugh). "I have no memory of that meeting. But we often meet our friends in strange places when we dream. And unless all dreamed alike, you must not ask them to remember it."

"Madam," said the Prince sternly, "I have already told your Grace that I am the King's son of Narnia."

"And shalt be, dear friend," said the Witch in a sooth-ing voice, as if she was humoring a child, "shalt be king of many imagined lands in thy fancies."

"We've been there, too," snapped Jill. She was very angry because she could feel enchantment getting hold of her every moment. But of course the very fact that she could still feel it, showed that it had not yet fully worked.

"And thou art Queen of Narnia too, I doubt not, pretty one," said the Witch in the same coaxing, half-mocking tone.

"I'm nothing of the sort," said Jill, stamping her foot. "*We* come from another world."

"Why, this is a prettier game than the other," said the Witch. "Tell us, little maid, where is this other world? What ships and chariots go between it and ours?"

Of course a lot of things darted into Jill's head at once: Experiment House, Adela Pennyfather, her own home, radio-sets, cinemas, cars, airplanes, ration-books, queues. But they seemed dim and far away. (*Thrum—thrum—thrum*—went the strings of the Witch's instrument.) Jill couldn't remember the names of the things in our world.

And this time it didn't come into her head that she was being enchanted, for now the magic was in its full strength; and of course, the more enchanted you get, the more you feel that you are not enchanted at all. She found herself saying (and at the moment it was a relief to say):

"No. I suppose that other world must be all a dream."

"Yes. It *is* all a dream," said the Witch, always thrumming.

"Yes, all a dream," said Jill.

"There never was such a world," said the Witch.

"No," said Jill and Scrubb, "never was such a world."

"There never was any world but mine," said the Witch.

"There never was any world but yours," said they.

Puddleglum was still fighting hard. "I don't know rightly what you all mean by a world," he said, talking like a man who hasn't enough air. "But you can play that fiddle till your fingers drop off, and still you won't make me forget Narnia; and the whole Overworld too. We'll never see it *again*, I shouldn't wonder. You may have blotted it out and turned it dark like this, for all I know. Nothing more likely. But I know I was there once. I've seen the sky

full of stars. I've seen the sun coming up out of the sea of a
morning and sinking behind the mountains at night. And
I've seen him up in the midday sky when I couldn't look at
him for brightness."

Puddleglum's words had a very rousing effect. The
other three all breathed again and looked at one another
like people newly awaked.

"Why, there it is!" cried the Prince. "Of course! The
blessing of Aslan upon this honest Marsh-wiggle. We have
all been dreaming, these last few minutes. How could we
have forgotten it? Of course we've all seen the sun."

"By Jove, so we have!" said Scrubb. "Good for you,
Puddleglum! You're the only one of us with any sense, I do
believe."

Then came the Witch's voice, cooing softly like the
voice of a wood-pigeon from the high elms in an old
garden at three o'clock in the middle of a sleepy, summer
afternoon; and it said:

"What is this *sun* that you all speak of? Do you mean
anything by the word?"

"Yes, we jolly well do," said Scrubb.

"Can you tell me what it's like?" asked the Witch (*thrum, thrum, thrum*, went the strings).

"Please it your Grace," said the Prince, very coldly and politely. "You see that lamp. It is round and yellow and gives light to the whole room; and hangeth moreover from the roof. Now that thing which we call the sun is like the lamp, only far greater and brighter. It giveth light to the whole Overworld and hangeth in the sky."

"Hangeth from what, my lord?" asked the Witch; and then, while they were all still thinking how to answer her, she added, with another of her soft, silver laughs: "You see? When you try to think out clearly what this *sun* must be, you cannot tell me. You can only tell me it is like the lamp. Your *sun* is a dream; and there is nothing in that dream that was not copied from the lamp. The lamp is the real thing—the *sun* is but a tale, a children's story."

"Yes, I see now," said Jill in a heavy, hopeless tone. "It must be so." And while she said this, it seemed to her to be very good sense.

Slowly and gravely the Witch repeated, "There is no *sun*." And they all said nothing. She repeated, in a softer and deeper voice. "There is no *sun*." After a pause, and after a struggle in their minds, all four of them said together, "You are right. There is no sun." It was such a relief to give in and say it.

"There never was a *sun*," said the Witch.

"No. There never was a sun," said the Prince, and the Marsh-wiggle, and the children.

For the last few minutes Jill had been feeling that there was something she must remember at all costs. And now she did. But it was dreadfully hard to say it. She felt as if huge weights were laid on her lips. At last, with an effort that seemed to take all the good out of her, she said:

"There's Aslan."

"Aslan?" said the Witch, quickening ever so slightly the pace of her thrumming. "What a pretty name! What does it mean?"

"He is the great Lion who called us out of our own world," said Scrubb, "and sent us into this to find Prince Rilian."

"What is a *lion*?" asked the Witch.

"Oh, hang it all!" said Scrubb. "Don't you know? How

can we describe it to her? Have you ever seen a cat?"

"Surely," said the Queen. "I love cats."

"Well, a lion is a little bit—only a little bit, mind you—like a huge cat—with a mane. At least, it's not like a horse's mane, you know, it's more like a judge's wig. And it's yellow. And terrifically strong."

The Witch shook her head. "I see," she said, "that we should do no better with your *lion*, as you call it, than we did with your *sun*. You have seen lamps, and so you imagined a bigger and better lamp and called it the *sun*. You've seen cats, and now you want a bigger and better cat, and it's to be called a *lion*. Well, 'tis a pretty make-believe, though, to say truth, it would suit you all better if you were younger. And look how you can put nothing into your make-believe without copying it from the real world, this world of mine, which is the only world. But even you children are too old for such play. As for you, my lord Prince, that art a man full grown, fie upon you! Are you not ashamed of such toys? Come, all of you. Put away these childish tricks. I have work for you all in the real world. There is no Narnia, no Overworld, no sky, no sun, no Aslan. And now, to bed all. And let us begin a wiser life tomorrow. But, first, to bed; to sleep; deep sleep, soft pillows, sleep without foolish dreams."

The Prince and the two children were standing with their heads hung down, their cheeks flushed, their eyes half closed; the strength all gone from them; the enchantment almost complete. But Puddleglum, desperately gathering all his strength, walked over to the fire. Then he did a very brave thing. He knew it wouldn't hurt him quite as much as it would hurt a human; for his feet (which were bare) were webbed and hard and cold-blooded like a duck's. But he knew it would hurt him badly enough; and so it did. With his bare foot he stamped on the fire, grinding a large part of it into ashes on the flat hearth. And three things happened at once.

First, the sweet, heavy smell grew very much less. For though the whole fire had not been put out, a good bit of it had, and what remained smelled very largely of burnt Marsh-wiggle, which is not at all an enchanting smell. This instantly made everyone's brain far clearer. The Prince and the children held up their heads again and opened their eyes.

Secondly, the Witch, in a loud, terrible voice, utterly different from all the sweet tones she had been using up till now, called out, "What are you doing? Dare to touch my fire again, mud-filth, and I'll turn the blood to fire inside your veins."

Thirdly, the pain itself made Puddleglum's head for a moment perfectly clear and he knew exactly what he really thought. There is nothing like a good shock of pain for dissolving certain kinds of magic.

"One word, Ma'am," he said, coming back from the fire; limping, because of the pain. "One word. All you've been saying is quite right, I shouldn't wonder. I'm a chap who always liked to know the worst and then put the best face I can on it. So I won't deny any of what you said. But there's one thing more to be said, even so. Suppose we *have* only dreamed, or made up, all those things—trees and grass and sun and moon and stars and Aslan himself. Suppose we have. Then all I can say is that, in that case, the made-up things seem a good deal more important than the real ones. Suppose this black pit of a kingdom of yours *is* the only world. Well, it strikes me as a pretty poor one. And that's a funny thing, when you come to think of it. We're just babies making up a game, if you're right. But four babies playing a game can make a play-world which licks your real world hollow. That's why I'm going to stand by the play-world. I'm on Aslan's side even if there isn't any Aslan to lead it. I'm going to live as like a Narnian as I can even if there isn't any Narnia. So, thanking you kindly for our supper, if these two gentlemen and the young lady are ready, we're leaving your court at once and setting out in the dark to spend our lives looking for Overland. Not that our lives will be very long, I should think; but that's a small loss if the world's as dull a place as you say."

"Oh, hurrah! Good old Puddleglum!" cried Scrubb and Jill. But the Prince shouted suddenly, "'Ware! Look to the Witch."

When they did look their hair nearly stood on end.

The instrument dropped from her hands. Her arms appeared to be fastened to her sides. Her legs were inter-twined with each other, and her feet had disappeared. The long green train of her skirt thickened and grew solid, and seemed to be all one piece with the writhing green pillar of her interlocked legs. And that writhing green pillar was curving and swaying as if it had no joints, or else were all joints. Her head was thrown far back and while her nose grew longer and longer, every other part of her face seemed to disappear, except her eyes. Huge flaming eyes they were now, without brows or lashes. All this takes time to write down; it happened so quickly that there was only just time to see it. Long before there was time to do anything, the change was complete, and the great serpent which the Witch had become, green as poison, thick as Jill's waist, had flung two or three coils of its loathsome body round the Prince's legs. Quick as lightning another great loop darted round, intending to pinion his sword-arm to his side. But the Prince was just in time. He raised his arms and got them clear: the living knot closed only round his chest—ready to crack his ribs like firewood when it drew tight.

The Prince caught the creature's neck in his left hand, trying to squeeze it till it choked. This held its face (if you could call it a face) about five inches from his own. The forked tongue flickered horribly in and out, but could not reach him. With his right hand he drew back his sword for the strongest blow he could give. Meanwhile Scrubb and Puddleglum had drawn their weapons and rushed to his aid. All three blows fell at once: Scrubb's (which did not even pierce the scales and did no good) on the body of the snake below the Prince's hand, but the Prince's own blow and Puddleglum's both on its neck. Even that did not quite kill it, though it began to loosen its hold on Rilian's legs and chest. With repeated blows they hacked off its head. The horrible thing went on coiling and moving like a bit of wire long after it had died; and the floor, as you may imagine, was a nasty mess.

The Prince, when he had breath, said, "Gentlemen, I thank you." Then the three conquerors stood staring at one another and panting, without another word, for a long time. Jill had very wisely sat down and was keeping quiet; she was saying to herself, "I do hope I don't faint—or blub—or do anything idiotic."

"My royal mother is avenged," said Rilian presently. "This is undoubtedly the same worm that I pursued in vain by the fountain in the forest of Narnia, so many years ago. All these years I have been the slave of my mother's slayer. Yet I am glad, gentlemen, that the foul Witch took to her serpent form at the last. It would not have suited well either with my heart or with my honor to have slain a woman. But look to the lady." He meant Jill.

"I'm all right, thanks," said she.

"Damsel," said the Prince, bowing to her. "You are of a high courage, and therefore, I doubt not, you come of a noble blood in your own world. But come, friends. Here is some wine left. Let us refresh ourselves and each pledge his fellows. After that, to our plans."

"A jolly good idea, Sir," said Scrubb.

Chapter Thirteen

Underland Without the Queen

ALL FELT THAT THEY HAD EARNED WHAT SCRUBB called a "breather." The Witch had locked the door and told the Earthmen not to disturb her, so there was no danger of interruption for the present. Their first business was, of course, Puddleglum's burnt foot. A couple of clean shirts from the Prince's bedroom, torn into strips, and well greased on the inside with butter and salad oil off the supper table, made a fairly good dressing. When this had been applied, they all sat down and had a little refreshment, and discussed plans for escaping from the Underworld.

Rilian explained that there were quite a lot of outlets by which one could get to the surface; he had been taken out through most of them at one time or another. But he had never gone out alone, only with the Witch; and he had always reached these outlets by going in a ship across the Sunless Sea. What the Earthmen would say if he went down to the harbor without the Witch, and with three strangers, and simply ordered a ship, no one could guess. But most likely they would ask awkward questions. On the other hand the new outlet, the one for the invasion of the Overworld, was on this side of the sea, and only a few miles away. The Prince knew that it was nearly finished; only a few feet of earth divided the diggings from the outer air. It was even possible that it had now been quite finished. Perhaps the Witch had come back to tell him this and to start the attack. Even if it was not, they could probably dig themselves out by that route in a few hours—if they could only get there without being stopped, and if

only they found the diggings unguarded. But those were
the difficulties.

"If you ask me—" began Puddleglum, when Scrubb
interrupted.

"I say," he asked, "what's that noise?"

"I've been wondering that for some time!" said Jill.

They had all, in fact, been hearing the noise but it had
begun and increased so gradually that they did not know
when they had first noticed it. For a time it had been only
a vague disquiet like gentle winds, or traffic very far away.
Then it swelled to a murmur like the sea. Then came rum-
blings and rushings. Now there seemed to be voices as well
and also a steady roaring that was not voices.

"By the Lion," said Prince Rilian, "it seems this silent
land has found a tongue at last." He rose, walked to the
window, and drew aside the curtains. The others crowded
round him to look out.

The very first thing they noticed was a great red glow.
Its reflection made a red patch on the roof of the Underworld thousands of feet above them, so that they could see
a rocky ceiling which had perhaps been hidden in dark-

ness ever since the world was made. The glow itself came from the far side of the city so that many buildings, grim and great, stood up blackly against it. But it also cast its light down many streets that ran from it toward the castle. And in those streets something very strange was going on. The closely-packed, silent crowds of Earthmen had vanished. Instead, there were figures darting about by ones, or twos, or threes. They behaved like people who do not want to be seen: lurking in shadow behind buttresses or in doorways, and then moving quickly across the open into fresh places of hiding. But the strangest thing of all, to anyone who knew the gnomes, was the noise. Shouts and cries came from all directions. But from the harbor there came a low, rumbling roar which grew steadily louder and was already shaking the whole city.

"What's happened to the Earthmen?" said Scrubb. "Is it *them* shouting?"

"'Tis hardly possible," said the Prince. "I never heard one of the rascals so much as speak with a loud voice in all the weary years of my bondage. Some new devilry, I don't doubt."

"And what is that red light over there?" asked Jill. "Is something on fire?"

"If you ask me," said Puddleglum, "I should say that was the central fires of the Earth breaking out to make a new volcano. We'll be in the middle of it, I shouldn't wonder."

"Look at that ship!" said Scrubb. "Why's it coming on so quickly? No one's rowing it."

"Look, look!" said the Prince. "The ship is already far this side of the harbor—it is in the street. Look! All the ships are driving into the city! By my head, the sea's rising. The flood is upon us. Aslan be praised, this castle stands on high ground. But the water comes on grimly fast."

"Oh, what *can* be happening?" cried Jill. "Fire and water and all those people dodging about the streets."

"I'll tell you what it is," said Puddleglum. "That Witch has laid a train of magic spells so that whenever she was killed, at that same moment her whole kingdom would fall to pieces. She's the sort that wouldn't so much mind dying herself if she knew that the chap who killed her was going to be burned, or buried, or drowned five minutes later."

"Hast hit it, friend wiggle," said the Prince. "When our swords hacked off the Witch's head, that stroke ended all her magic works, and now the Deep Lands are falling to pieces. We are looking on the end of the Underworld."

"That's it, Sir," said Puddleglum. "Unless it should happen to be the end of the whole world."

"But are we just going to stay here and—wait?" gasped Jill.

"Not by my counsel," said the Prince. "I would save my horse, Coalblack, and the Witch's Snowflake (a noble beast and worthy of a better mistress) which are both stabled in the courtyard. After that, let us make shift to get out to high ground and pray that we shall find an outlet. The horses can carry two each at need, and if we put them to it they may outstrip the flood."

"Will your Highness not put on armor?" asked Puddleglum. "I don't like the look of *those*"—and he pointed down to the street. Everyone looked down. Dozens of creatures (and now that they were close, they obviously were Earthmen) were coming up from the direction of the harbor. But they were not moving like an aimless crowd. They behaved like modern soldiers in an attack, making rushes and taking cover, anxious not to be seen from the castle windows.

"I dare not see the inside of that armor again," said the Prince. "I rode in it as in a movable dungeon, and it stinks of magic and slavery. But I will take the shield."

He left the room and returned with a strange light in his eyes a moment later.

"Look, friends," he said, holding out the shield toward them. "An hour ago it was black and without device; and now, this." The shield had turned bright as silver, and on it, redder than blood or cherries, was the figure of the Lion.

"Doubtless," said the Prince, "this signifies that Aslan will be our good lord, whether he means us to live or die. And all's one, for that. Now, by my counsel, we shall all kneel and kiss his likeness, and then all shake hands one with another, as true friends that may shortly be parted. And then, let us descend into the city and take the adventure that is sent us."

And they all did as the Prince had said. But when Scrubb shook hands with Jill, he said, "So long, Jill. Sorry

I've been a funk and so ratty. I hope you get safe home," and Jill said, "So long, Eustace. And I'm sorry I've been such a pig." And this was the first time they had ever used Christian names, because one didn't do it at school.

The Prince unlocked the door and they all went down the stairs: three of them with drawn swords, and Jill with drawn knife. The attendants had vanished and the great room at the foot of the Prince's stairs was empty. The gray, doleful lamps were still burning and by their light they had no difficulty in passing gallery after gallery and descending stairway after stairway. The noises from outside the castle were not so easily heard here as they had been in the room above. Inside the house all was still as death, and deserted. It was as they turned a corner into the great hall on the ground floor that they met their first Earthman—a fat, whitish creature with a very piglike face who was gobbling up all the remains of food on the tables. It squealed (the squeal also was very like a pig's) and darted under a bench, whisking its long tail out of Puddleglum's reach in the nick of time. Then it rushed away through the far door too quickly to be followed.

From the hall they came out into the courtyard. Jill, who went to a riding school in the holidays, had just noticed the smell of a stable (a very nice, honest, homely smell it is to meet in a place like Underland) when Eustace said, "Great Scott! Look at that!" A magnificent rocket had risen from somewhere beyond the castle walls and broken into green stars.

"Fireworks!" said Jill in a puzzled voice.

"Yes," said Eustace, "but you can't imagine those Earth people letting them off for fun! It must be a signal."

"And means no good to us, I'll be bound," said Puddleglum.

"Friends," said the Prince, "when once a man is launched on such an adventure as this, he must bid farewell to hopes and fears, otherwise death or deliverance will both come too late to save his honor and his reason. Ho, my beauties" (he was now opening the stable door). "Hey, cousins! Steady, Coalblack! Softly now, Snowflake! You are not forgotten."

The horses were both frightened by the strange lights and the noises. Jill, who had been so cowardly about going through a black hole between one cave and another, went in without fear between the stamping and snorting beasts, and she and the Prince had them saddled and bridled in a few minutes. Very fine they looked as they came out into the courtyard, tossing their heads. Jill mounted Snowflake, and Puddleglum got up behind her. Eustace got up behind the Prince on Coalblack. Then with a great echo of hoofs, they rode out of the main gateway into the street.

"Not much danger of being burnt. That's the bright side of it," observed Puddleglum, pointing to their right. There, hardly a hundred yards away, lapping against the walls of the houses, was water.

"Courage!" said the Prince. "The road there goes down steeply. That water has climbed only half up the greatest hill in the city. It might come so near in the first half-hour and come no nearer in the next two. My fear is more of that—" and he pointed with his sword to a great tall Earthman with boar's tusks, followed by six others of assorted shapes and sizes who had just dashed out of a side street and stepped into the shadow of the houses where no one could see them.

The Prince led them, aiming always in the direction of the glowing red light but a little to the left of it. His plan was to get round the fire (if it was a fire) on to high ground, in hopes that they might find their way to the new diggings. Unlike the other three, he seemed to be almost enjoying himself. He whistled as he rode, and sang snatches of an old song about Corin Thunder-fist of Archenland. The truth is, he was so glad at being free from his long enchantment that all dangers seemed a game in comparison. But the rest found it an eerie journey.

Behind them was the sound of clashing and entangled ships, and the rumble of collapsing buildings. Overhead was the great patch of lurid light on the roof of the Underworld. Ahead was the mysterious glow, which did not seem to grow any bigger. From the same direction came the continual hubbub of shouts, screams, cat-calls, laughter, squeals, and bellowings; and fireworks of all sorts rose in the dark air. No one could guess what they meant. Nearer to them, the city was partly lit up by the red glow, and partly by the very different light of the dreary Gnome lamps. But there were many places where neither of these lights fell, and those places were jet-black. And in and out of those places the shapes of Earthmen were darting and slipping all the time, always with their eyes fixed on the travelers, always trying to keep out of sight themselves. There were big and little faces, huge eyes like fishes' eyes and little eyes like bears'. There were feathers and bristles, horns and tusks, noses like whipcord and chins so long that they looked like beards. Every now and then a group of them would get too big or come too near. Then the Prince would brandish his sword and make a show of charging them. And the creatures, with all manner of hootings, squeakings, and cluckings, would dive away into the darkness.

But when they had climbed many steep streets and were far away from the flood, and almost out of the town on the inland side, it began to be more serious. They were now close to the red glow and nearly on a level with it, though they still could not see what it really was. But by its light they could see their enemies more clearly. Hundreds—perhaps a few thousands—of gnomes were all moving toward it. But they were doing so in short rushes, and whenever they stopped, they turned and faced the travelers.

"If your Highness asked me," said Puddleglum, "I'd say those fellows were meaning to cut us off in front."

"That was my thought too, Puddleglum," said the Prince. "And we can never fight our way through so many. Hark you! Let us ride forth close by the edge of yonder house. And even as we reach it, do you slip off into its shadow. The Lady and I will go forward a few paces. Some of these devils will follow us, I doubt not; they are thick behind us. Do you, who have long arms, take one alive if you may, as it passes your ambush. We may get a true tale of it or learn what is their quarrel against us."

"But won't the others all come rushing at us to rescue the one we catch," said Jill in a voice not so steady as she tried to make it.

"Then, Madam," said the Prince, "you shall see us die fighting around you, and you must commend yourself to the Lion. Now, good Puddleglum."

The Marsh-wiggle slipped off into the shadow as quickly as a cat. The others, for a sickening minute or so, went forward at a walk. Then suddenly from behind them there broke out a series of blood-curdling screams, mixed with the familiar voice of Puddleglum, saying, "Now then! Don't cry out before you're hurt, or you *will* be hurt, see? Anyone would think it was a pig being killed."

"That was good hunting," exclaimed the Prince, immediately turning Coalblack and coming back to the corner of the house. "Eustace," he said, "of your courtesy, take Coalblack's head." Then he dismounted, and all three gazed in silence while Puddleglum pulled his catch out into the light. It was a most miserable little gnome, only about three feet long. It had a sort of ridge, like a cock's comb (only hard), on the top of its head, little pink eyes, and a mouth and chin so large and round that its face looked like that of a pigmy hippopotamus. If they had not been in such a tight place, they would have burst into laughter at the sight of it.

"Now, Earthman," said the Prince, standing over it and holding his sword point very near the prisoner's neck, "speak up, like an honest gnome, and you shall go free. Play the knave with us, and you are but a dead Earthman. Good Puddleglum, how can it speak while you hold its mouth tight shut?"

"No, and it can't bite either," said Puddleglum. "If I had the silly soft hands that you humans have (saving your Highness's reverence) I'd have been all over blood by now. Yet even a Marsh-wiggle gets tired of being chewed."

"Sirrah," said the Prince to the gnome, "one bite and you die. Let its mouth open, Puddleglum."

"Oo-ee-ee," squealed the Earthman. "Let me go, let me go. It isn't me. I didn't do it."

"Didn't do what?" asked Puddleglum.

"Whatever your Honors say I *did* do," answered the creature.

"Tell me your name," said the Prince, "and what you Earthmen are all about today."

"Oh please, your Honors, please, kind gentlemen," whimpered the gnome. "Promise you will not tell the Queen's grace anything I say."

"The Queen's grace, as you call her," said the Prince sternly, "is dead. I killed her myself."

"What!" cried the gnome, opening its ridiculous mouth wider and wider in astonishment. "Dead? The Witch dead? And by your Honor's hand?" It gave a huge sigh of relief and added, "Why then your Honor is a friend!"

The Prince withdrew his sword an inch or so. Puddleglum let the creature sit up. It looked round on the four travelers with its twinkling, red eyes, chuckled once or twice, and began.

Chapter Fourteen

The Bottom of the World

"MY NAME IS GOLG," SAID THE GNOME. "AND I'LL
tell your Honors all I know. About an hour ago we were all
going about our work—*her* work, I should say—sad and
silent, same as we've done any other day for years and years.
Then there came a great crash and bang. As soon as they
heard it, everyone says to himself, I haven't had a song
or a dance or let off a squib for a long time; why's that?
And everyone thinks to himself, Why, I must have been

enchanted. And then everyone says to himself, I'm blessed if I know why I'm carrying this load, and I'm not going to carry it any farther: that's that. And down we all throw our sacks and bundles and tools. Then everyone turns and sees the great red glow over yonder. And everyone says to himself, What's that? And everyone answers himself and says, There's a crack or chasm split open and a nice warm glow coming up through it from the Really Deep Land, a thousand fathom under us."

"Great Scott," exclaimed Eustace, "are there other lands still lower down?"

"Oh yes, your Honor," said Golg. "Lovely places; what we call the Land of Bism. This country where we are now, the Witch's country, is what *we* call the Shallow Lands. It's a good deal too near the surface to suit us. Ugh! You might almost as well be living outside, on the surface itself. You see, we're all poor gnomes from Bism whom the Witch has called up here by magic to work for her. But we'd forgotten all about it till that crash came and the spell broke. We didn't know who we were or where we belonged. We couldn't do anything, or think anything, except what she put into our heads. And it was glum and gloomy things she put there all those years. I've nearly forgotten how to make a joke or dance a jig. But the moment the bang came and the chasm opened and the sea began rising, it all came back. And of course we all set off as quick as we could to get down the crack and home to our own place. And you can see them over there all letting off rockets and standing on their heads for joy. And I'll be very obliged to your Honors if you'll soon let me go and join in."

"I think this is simply splendid," said Jill. "I'm so glad we freed the gnomes as well as ourselves when we cut off the Witch's head! And I'm so glad they aren't really horrid and gloomy any more than the Prince really was—well, what he seemed like."

"That's all very well, Pole," said Puddleglum cautiously. "But those gnomes didn't look to me like chaps who were just running away. It looked more like military formations, if you ask me. Do you look me in the face, Mr. Golg, and tell me you weren't preparing for battle?"

"Of course we were, your Honor," said Golg. "You see, we didn't know the Witch was dead. We thought she'd be watching from the castle. We were trying to slip away without being seen. And then when you four came out with swords and horses, of course everyone says to himself, Here it comes: not knowing that his Honor wasn't on the Witch's side. And we were determined to fight like anything rather than give up the hope of going back to Bism."

"I'll be sworn 'tis an honest gnome," said the Prince. "Let go of it, friend Puddleglum. As for me, good Golg, I have been enchanted like you and your fellows, and have but newly remembered myself. And now, one question more. Do you know the way to those new diggings, by which the sorceress meant to lead out an army against Overland?"

"Ee-ee-ee!" squeaked Golg. "Yes, I know that terrible road. I will show you where it begins. But it is no manner of use your Honor asking me to go with you on it. I'll die rather."

"Why?" asked Eustace anxiously. "What's so dreadful about it?"

"Too near the top, the outside," said Golg, shuddering. "That was the worst thing the Witch did to us. We were going to be led out into the open—into the outside of the world. They say there's no roof at all there; only a horrible, great emptiness called the sky. And the diggings have gone so far that a few strokes of the pick would bring you out to it. I wouldn't dare go near them."

"Hurrah! Now you're talking!" cried Eustace, and Jill said, "But it's not horrid at all up there. We like it. We live there."

"I know you Overlanders live there," said Golg. "But I thought it was because you couldn't find your way down inside. You can't really *like* it—crawling about like flies on top of the world!"

"What about showing us the road at once?" said Puddleglum.

"In a good hour," cried the Prince. The whole party set out. The Prince remounted his charger, Puddleglum climbed up behind Jill, and Golg led the way. As he went, he kept shouting out the good news that the Witch was dead and that the four Overlanders were not dangerous. And those who heard him shouted it on to others, so that in a few minutes the whole of Underland was ringing with

shouts and cheers, and gnomes by hundreds and thousands, leaping, turning cart-wheels, standing on their
heads, playing leap-frog, and letting off huge crackers,
came pressing round Coalblack and Snowflake. And the
Prince had to tell the story of his own enchantment and
deliverance at least ten times.

In this way they came to the edge of the chasm. It was
about a thousand feet long and perhaps two hundred wide.
They dismounted from their horses and came to the edge,
and looked down into it. A strong heat smote up into their
faces, mixed with a smell which was quite unlike any they
had ever smelled. It was rich, sharp, exciting, and made you
sneeze. The depth of the chasm was so bright that at first it
dazzled their eyes and they could see nothing. When they
got used to it they thought they could make out a river of fire,
and, on the banks of that river, what seemed to be fields and
groves of an unbearable, hot brilliance—though they were
dim compared with the river. There were blues, reds, greens,
and whites all jumbled together: a very good stained-glass
window with the tropical sun staring straight through it at
midday might have something of the same effect. Down the
rugged sides of the chasm, looking black like flies against all

that fiery light, hundreds of Earthmen were climbing.

"Your Honors," said Golg (and when they turned to look at him they could see nothing but blackness for a few minutes, their eyes were so dazzled). "Your Honors, why don't you come down to Bism? You'd be happier there than in that cold, unprotected, naked country out on top. Or at least come down for a short visit."

Jill took it for granted that none of the others would listen to such an idea for a moment. To her horror she heard the Prince saying:

"Truly, friend Golg, I have half a mind to come down with you. For this is a marvelous adventure, and it may be no mortal man has ever looked into Bism before or will ever have the chance again. And I know not how, as the years pass, I shall bear to remember that it was once in my power to have probed the uttermost pit of Earth and that I forbore. But could a man live there? You do not swim in the fire-river itself?"

"Oh no, your Honor. Not we. It's only salamanders live in the fire itself."

"What kind of beast is your salamander?" asked the Prince.

"It is hard to tell their kind, your Honor," said Golg. "For they are too white-hot to look at. But they are most like small dragons. They speak to us out of the fire. They are wonderfully clever with their tongues: very witty and eloquent."

Jill glanced hastily at Eustace. She had felt sure that he would like the idea of sliding down that chasm even less than she did. Her heart sank as she saw that his face was quite changed. He looked much more like the Prince than like the old Scrubb at Experiment House. For all his adventures, and the days when he had sailed with King Caspian, were coming back to him.

"Your Highness," he said. "If my old friend Reepicheep the Mouse were here, he would say we could not now refuse the adventures of Bism without a great impeachment to our honor."

"Down there," said Golg, "I could show you real gold, real silver, real diamonds."

"Bosh!" said Jill rudely. "As if we didn't know that we're below the deepest mines even here."

"Yes," said Golg. "I have heard of those little scratches in the crust that you Topdwellers call mines. But that's where you get dead gold, dead silver, dead gems. Down in Bism we have them alive and growing. There I'll pick you bunches of rubies that you can eat and squeeze you a cupful of diamond juice. You won't care much about fingering the cold, dead treasures of your shallow mines after you have tasted the live ones in Bism."

"My father went to the world's end," said Rilian thoughtfully. "It would be a marvelous thing if his son went to the bottom of the world."

"If your Highness wants to see your father while he's still alive, which I think he'd prefer," said Puddleglum, "it's about time we were getting onto that road to the diggings."

"And I won't go down that hole, whatever anyone says," added Jill.

"Why, if your Honors are really set to go back to Overworld," said Golg, "there *is* one bit of the road that's rather lower than this. And perhaps, if that flood's still rising—"

"Oh, do, do, do come *on!*" begged Jill.

"I fear it must be so," said the Prince with a deep sigh. "But I have left half of my heart in the land of Bism."

"Please!" begged Jill.

"Where is the road?" asked Puddleglum.

"There are lamps all the way," said Golg. "Your Honor can see the beginning of the road on the far side of the chasm."

"How long will the lamps burn for?" asked Puddleglum.

At that moment a hissing, scorching voice like the voice of Fire itself (they wondered afterward if it could have been a salamander's) came whistling up out of the very depths of Bism.

"Quick! Quick! Quick! To the cliffs, to the cliffs, to the cliffs!" it said. "The rift closes. It closes. It closes. Quick! Quick!" And at the same time, with ear-shattering cracks and creaks, the rocks moved. Already, while they looked, the chasm was narrower. From every side belated gnomes were rushing into it. They would not wait to climb down the rocks. They flung themselves headlong and, either because so strong a blast of hot air was beating up from the bottom, or for some other reason, they could be seen floating downward like leaves. Thicker and thicker they floated, till their blackness almost blotted out the fiery river and the groves of live gems. "Good-bye to your Honors. I'm off," shouted Golg, and dived. Only a few were left to follow him. The chasm was now no broader than a stream. Now it was narrow as the slit in a pillar box. Now it was only an intensely bright thread. Then, with a shock like a thousand goods trains crashing into a thousand pairs of buffers, the lips of rock closed. The hot, maddening smell vanished. The travelers were alone in an Underworld which now looked far blacker than before. Pale, dim, and dreary, the lamps marked the direction of the road.

"Now," said Puddleglum, "it's ten to one we've already stayed too long, but we may as well make a try. Those lamps will give out in five minutes, I shouldn't wonder."

They urged the horses to a canter and thundered along the dusky road in fine style. But almost at once it began going downhill. They would have thought Golg had sent them the wrong way if they had not seen, on the other side of the valley, the lamps going on and upward as far as the eye could reach. But at the bottom of the valley the lamps shone on moving water.

"Haste," cried the Prince. They galloped down the

slope. It would have been nasty enough at the bottom even five minutes later for the tide was running up the valley like a mill-race, and if it had come to swimming, the horses could hardly have won over. But it was still only a foot or two deep, and though it swished terribly round the horses' legs, they reached the far side in safety.

Then began the slow, weary march uphill with nothing ahead to look at but the pale lamps which went up and up as far as the eye could reach. When they looked back they could see the water spreading. All the hills of Underland were now islands, and it was only on those islands that the lamps remained. Every moment some distant light vanished. Soon there would be total darkness everywhere except on the road they were following; and even on the lower part of it behind them, though no lamps had yet gone out, the lamplight shone on water.

Although they had good reason for hurrying, the horses could not go on forever without a rest. They halted: and in silence they could hear the lapping of water.

"I wonder is what's his name—Father Time—flooded out now," said Jill. "And all those queer sleeping animals."

"I don't think we're as high as that," said Eustace. "Don't you remember how we had to go downhill to reach the sunless sea? I shouldn't think the water has reached Father Time's cave yet."

"That's as may be," said Puddleglum. "I'm more interested in the lamps on this road. Look a bit sickly, don't they?"

"They always did," said Jill.

"Ah," said Puddleglum. "But they're greener now."

"You don't mean to say you think they're going out?" cried Eustace.

"Well, however they work, you can't expect them to last forever, you know," replied the Marsh-wiggle. "But don't let your spirits down, Scrubb. I've got my eye on the water too, and I don't think it's rising so fast as it did."

"Small comfort, friend," said the Prince. "If we cannot find our way out. I cry you mercy, all. I am to blame for my pride and fantasy which delayed us by the mouth of the land of Bism. Now, let us ride on."

During the hour or so that followed Jill sometimes thought that Puddleglum was right about the lamps, and sometimes thought it was only her imagination. Meanwhile, the land was changing. The roof of Underland was so near that even by that dull light they could now see it quite distinctly. And the great, rugged walls of Underland could be seen drawing closer on each side. The road, in fact, was leading them up into a steep tunnel. They began to pass picks and shovels and barrows and other signs that the diggers had recently been at work. If only one could be sure of getting out, all this was very cheering. But the thought of going on into a hole that would get narrower and narrower, and harder to turn back in, was very unpleasant.

At last the roof was so low that Puddleglum and the Prince knocked their heads against it. The party dismounted and led the horses. The road was uneven here and one had to pick one's steps with some care. That was how Jill noticed the growing darkness. There was no doubt about it now. The faces of the others looked strange and ghastly in the green glow. Then all at once (she couldn't help it) Jill gave a little scream. One light, the next one ahead, went out altogether. The one behind them did the same. Then they were in absolute darkness.

"Courage, friends," came Prince Rilian's voice. "Whether we live or die Aslan will be our good lord."

"That's right, Sir," said Puddleglum's voice. "And you must always remember there's one good thing about being trapped down here: it'll save funeral expenses."

Jill held her tongue. (If you don't want other people to know how frightened you are, this is always a wise thing to do; it's your voice that gives you away.)

"We might as well go on as stand here," said Eustace; and when she heard the tremble in *his* voice, Jill knew how wise she'd been not to trust her own.

Puddleglum and Eustace went first with their arms stretched out in front of them, for fear of blundering into anything; Jill and the Prince followed, leading the horses.

"I say," came Eustace's voice much later, "are my eyes going queer, or is there a patch of light up there?"

Before anyone could answer him, Puddleglum called out: "Stop. I'm up against a dead end. And it's earth, not rock. What were you saying, Scrubb?"

"By the Lion," said the Prince, "Eustace is right. There is a sort of—"

"But it's not daylight," said Jill. "It's only a cold blue sort of light."

"Better than nothing, though," said Eustace. "Can we get up to it?"

"It's not right overhead," said Puddleglum. "It's above us, but it's in this wall that I've run into. How would it be, Pole, if you got on my shoulders and saw whether you could get up to it?"

Chapter Fifteen

The Disappearance
of Jill

THE PATCH OF LIGHT DID NOT SHOW UP ANYTHING down in the darkness where they were standing. The others could only hear, not see, Jill's efforts to get onto the Marsh-wiggle's back. That is, they heard him saying, "You needn't put your finger in my eye," and, "Nor your foot in my mouth either," and, "That's more like it," and, "Now, I'll hold on to your legs. That'll leave your arms free to steady yourself against the earth."

Then they looked up and soon they saw the black shape of Jill's head against the patch of light.

"Well?" they all shouted up anxiously.

"It's a hole," called Jill's voice. "I could get through it if I was a bit higher."

"What do you see through it?" asked Eustace.

"Nothing much yet," said Jill. "I say, Puddleglum, let go my legs so that I can stand on your shoulders instead of sitting on them. I can steady myself all right against the edge."

They could hear her moving and then much more of her came into sight against the grayness of the opening; in fact all of her down to the waist.

"I say—" began Jill, but suddenly broke off with a cry: not a sharp cry. It sounded more as if her mouth had been muffled up or had something pushed into it. After that she found her voice and seemed to be shouting out as loud as she could, but they couldn't hear the words. Two things then happened at the same moment. The patch of light was completely blocked up for a second or so; and they heard both a scuffling, struggling sound and the voice of the Marsh-wiggle gasping: "Quick! Help! Hold on to her legs. Someone's pulling her. There! No, here. Too late!"

The opening, and the cold light which filled it, were now perfectly clear again. Jill had vanished.

"Jill! Jill!" they shouted frantically, but there was no answer.

"Why the dickens couldn't you have held her feet?" said Eustace.

"I don't know, Scrubb," groaned Puddleglum. "Born to be a misfit, I shouldn't wonder. Fated. Fated to be Pole's death, just as I was fated to eat Talking Stag at Harfang. Not that it isn't my own fault as well, of course."

"This is the greatest shame and sorrow that could have fallen on us," said the Prince. "We have sent a brave lady into the hands of enemies and stayed behind in safety."

"Don't paint it *too* black, Sir," said Puddleglum. "We're not very safe except for death by starvation in this hole."

"I wonder, am *I* small enough to get through where Jill did?" said Eustace.

What had really happened to Jill was this. As soon as she got her head out of the hole she found that she was looking down as if from an upstairs window, not up as if through a trap-door. She had been so long in the dark that her eyes couldn't at first take in what they were seeing: except that she was not looking at the daylit, sunny world which she so wanted to see. The air seemed to be deadly cold, and the light was pale and blue. There was also a good deal of noise going on and a lot of white objects flying about in the air. It was at that moment that she had shouted down to Puddleglum to let her stand on his shoulders.

When she had done this, she could see and hear a good deal better. The noises she had been hearing turned out to be two kinds: the rhythmical thump of several feet, and the music of four fiddles, three flutes, and a drum. She also got her own position clear. She was looking out of a hole in a steep bank which sloped down and reached the level about fourteen feet below her. Everything was very white. A lot of people were moving about. Then she gasped! The people were trim little Fauns, and Dryads with leaf-crowned hair floating behind them. For a second they looked as if they were moving anyhow; then she saw that they were really doing a dance—a dance with so many complicated steps and figures that it took you some time

to understand it. Then it came over her like a thunderclap
that the pale, blue light was moonlight, and the white stuff
on the ground was really snow. And of course! There were
the stars staring in a black frosty sky overhead. And the tall
black things behind the dancers were trees. They had not
only got out into the upper world at last, but had come out
in the heart of Narnia. Jill felt she could have fainted with
delight; and the music—the wild music, intensely sweet
and yet just the least bit eerie too, and full of good magic as
the Witch's thrumming had been full of bad magic—
made her feel it all the more.

All this takes a long time to tell, but of course it took a
very short time to see. Jill turned almost at once to shout
down to the others, "I say! It's all right. We're out, and we're
home." But the reason she never got further than "I say"
was this. Circling round and round the dancers was a ring
of Dwarfs, all dressed in their finest clothes; mostly scarlet
with fur-lined hoods and golden tassels and big furry
top-boots. As they circled round they were all diligently
throwing snowballs. (Those were the white things that Jill
had seen flying through the air.) They weren't throwing

them *at* the dancers as silly boys might have been doing in England. They were throwing them through the dance in such perfect time with the music and with such perfect aim that if all the dancers were in exactly the right places at exactly the right moments, no one would be hit. This is called the Great Snow Dance and is done every year in Narnia on the first moonlit night when there is snow on the ground. Of course it is a kind of game as well as a dance, because every now and then some dancer will be the least little bit wrong and get a snowball in the face, and then everyone laughs. But a good team of dancers, Dwarfs, and musicians will keep it up for hours without a single hit. On fine nights when the cold and the drum-taps, and the hooting of the owls, and the moonlight, have got into their wild, woodland blood and made it even wilder, they will dance till daybreak. I wish you could see it for yourselves.

What had stopped Jill when she got as far as the *say* of "I say" was of course simply a fine big snowball that came sailing through the dance from a Dwarf on the far side and got her fair and square in the mouth. She didn't in the least mind; twenty snowballs would not have damped her spirits at that moment. But however happy you are feeling, you can't talk with your mouth full of snow. And when, after considerable spluttering, she could speak again, she quite forgot in her excitement that the others, down in the dark, behind her, still didn't know the good news. She simply leaned as far out of the hole as she could, and yelled to the dancers.

"Help! Help! We're buried in the hill. Come and dig us out."

The Narnians, who had not even noticed the little hole in the hillside, were of course very surprised, and looked about in several wrong directions before they found out where the voice was coming from. But when they caught sight of Jill they all came running toward her, and as many as could scrambled up the bank, and a dozen or more hands were stretched up to help her. And Jill caught hold of them and thus got out of the hole and came slithering down the bank head first, and then picked herself up and said:

"Oh, do go and dig the others out. There are three others, besides the horses. And one of them is Prince Rilian."

She was already in the middle of a crowd when she said this, for besides the dancers all sorts of people who had been watching the dance, and whom she had not seen at first, came running up. Squirrels came out of the trees in showers, and so did Owls. Hedgehogs came waddling as fast as their short legs would carry them. Bears and Badgers followed at a slower pace. A great Panther, twitching its tail in excitement, was the last to join the party.

But as soon as they understood what Jill was saying, they all became active. "Pick and shovel, boys, pick and shovel. Off for our tools!" said the Dwarfs, and dashed away into the woods at top speed. "Wake up some Moles, they're the chaps for digging. They're quite as good as Dwarfs," said a voice. "What was that she said about Prince Rilian?" said another. "Hush!" said the Panther. "The poor child's crazed, and no wonder after being lost inside the hill. She doesn't know what she's saying." "That's right," said an old Bear. "Why, she said Prince Rilian was a horse!"—"No, she didn't," said a Squirrel, very pert. "Yes, she did," said another Squirrel, even perter.

"It's quite t-t-t-true. D-d-don't be so silly," said Jill. She spoke like that because her teeth were now chattering with the cold.

Immediately one of the Dryads flung round her a furry cloak which some Dwarf had dropped when he rushed to fetch his mining tools, and an obliging Faun trotted off among the trees to a place where Jill could see firelight in the mouth of a cave, to get her a hot drink. But before it came, all the Dwarfs reappeared with spades and pickaxes and charged at the hillside. Then Jill heard cries of "Hi! What are you doing? Put that sword down," and "Now, young 'un: none of that," and, "He's a vicious one, now, isn't he?" Jill hurried to the spot and didn't know whether to laugh or cry when she saw Eustace's face, very pale and dirty, projecting from the blackness of the hole, and Eustace's right hand brandishing a sword with which he made lunges at anyone who came near him.

For of course Eustace had been having a very different time from Jill during the last few minutes. He had heard Jill cry out and seen her disappear into the unknown. Like the Prince and Puddleglum, he thought that some enemies had caught her. And from down below he didn't see that the pale, bluish light was moonlight. He thought the hole would lead only into some other cave, lit by some ghostly phosphorescence and filled with goodness-knows-what evil creatures of the Underworld. So that when he had persuaded Puddleglum to give him a back, and drawn his sword, and poked out his head, he had really been doing a very brave thing. The others would have done it first if they could, but the hole was too small for them to climb through. Eustace was a little bigger, and a lot clumsier, than Jill, so that when he looked out he bumped his head against the top of the hole and brought a small avalanche of snow down on his face. And so, when he could see again, and saw a dozen of figures coming at him as hard as they could run, it is not surprising that he tried to ward them off.

"Stop, Eustace, stop!" cried Jill. "They're all friends. Can't you see? We've come up in Narnia. Everything's all right."

Then Eustace did see, and apologized to the Dwarfs (and the Dwarfs said not to mention it), and dozens of thick, hairy, dwarfish hands helped him out just as they had helped Jill out a few minutes before. Then Jill scrambled up the bank and put her head in at the dark opening and shouted the good news in to the prisoners. As she turned away she heard Puddleglum mutter, "Ah, poor Pole. It's been too much for her, this last bit. Turned her head, I shouldn't wonder. She's beginning to see things."

Jill rejoined Eustace and they shook one another by both hands and took in great deep breaths of the free midnight air. And a warm cloak was brought for Eustace and hot drinks, for both. While they were sipping it, the Dwarfs had already got all the snow and all the sods off a large strip of the hillside round the original hole, and the pick-axes and spades were now going as merrily as the feet of Fauns and Dryads had been going in the dance ten minutes before. Only ten minutes! Yet already it felt to Jill and Eustace as if all their dangers in the dark and heat and general smotheriness of the earth must have been only a dream. Out here, in the cold, with the moon and the huge stars overhead (Narnian stars are nearer than stars in our world) and with kind, merry faces all round them, one couldn't quite believe in Underland.

Before they had finished their hot drinks, a dozen or so

Moles, newly waked and still very sleepy, and not well pleased, had arrived. But as soon as they understood what it was all about, they joined in with a will. Even the Fauns made themselves useful by carting away the earth in little barrows, and the Squirrels danced and leaped to and fro in great excitement, though Jill never found out exactly what they thought they were doing. The Bears and Owls contented themselves with giving advice, and kept on asking the children if they wouldn't like to come into the cave (that was where Jill had seen the firelight) and get warm and have supper. But the children couldn't bear to go without seeing their friends set free.

No one in our world can work at a job of that sort as Dwarfs and Talking Moles work in Narnia; but then, of course, Moles and Dwarfs don't look on it as work. They like digging. It was therefore not really long before they had opened a great black chasm in the hillside. And out from the blackness into the moonlight—this would have been rather dreadful if one hadn't known who they were—came, first, the long, leggy, steeple-hatted figure of the Marsh-wiggle, and then, leading two great horses,

Rilian the Prince himself.

As Puddleglum appeared shouts broke out on every side: "Why, it's a Wiggle—why, it's old Puddleglum—old Puddleglum from the Eastern Marshes—what ever have you been doing, Puddleglum?—there've been search-parties out for you—the Lord Trumpkin has been putting up notices—there's a reward offered!" But all this died away, all in one moment, into dead silence, as quickly as the noise dies away in a rowdy dormitory if the Headmaster opens the door. For now they saw the Prince.

No one doubted for a moment who he was. There were plenty of Beasts and Dryads and Dwarfs and Fauns who remembered him from the days before his enchanting. There were some old ones who could just remember how his father, King Caspian, had looked when he was a young man, and saw the likeness. But I think they would have known him anyway. Pale though he was from long imprisonment in the Deep Lands, dressed in black, dusty, disheveled, and weary, there was something in his face and air which no one could mistake. That look is in the face of all true Kings of Narnia, who rule by the will of Aslan and sit at Cair Paravel on the throne of Peter the High King. Instantly every head was bared and every knee was bent; a moment later such cheering and shouting, such jumps and reels of joy, such hand-shakings and kissings and embracings of everybody by everybody else broke out that the tears came into Jill's eyes. Their quest had been worth all the pains it cost.

"Please it your Highness," said the oldest of the Dwarfs, "there is some attempt at a supper in the cave yonder, prepared against the ending of the snow-dance—"

"With a good will, Father," said the Prince. "For never had any Prince, Knight, Gentleman, or Bear so good a stomach to his victuals as we four wanderers have tonight."

The whole crowd began to move away through the trees toward the cave. Jill heard Puddleglum saying to those who pressed round him, "No, no, my story can wait. Nothing worth talking about has happened to me. I want to hear the news. Don't try breaking it to me gently, for I'd rather have it all at once. Has the King been shipwrecked? Any forest fires? No wars on the Calormen border? Or a few dragons, I shouldn't wonder?" And all the creatures laughed aloud and said, "Isn't that just like a Marsh-wiggle?"

The two children were nearly dropping with tiredness and hunger, but the warmth of the cave, and the very sight of it, with the firelight dancing on the walls and dressers and cups and saucers and plates and on the smooth stone floor, just as it does in a farmhouse kitchen, revived them a little. All the same they went fast asleep while supper was being got ready. And while they slept Prince Rilian was talking over the whole adventure with the older and wiser Beasts and Dwarfs. And now they all saw what it meant; how a wicked Witch (doubtless the same kind as that White Witch who had brought the Great Winter on Narnia long ago) had contrived the whole thing, first killing Rilian's mother and enchanting Rilian himself. And they saw how she had dug right under Narnia and was going to break out and rule it through Rilian: and how he had never dreamed that the country of which she would make him king (king in name, but really her slave) was his own country. And from the children's part of the story they saw how she was in league and friendship with the dangerous giants of Harfang. "And the lesson of it all is, your Highness," said the oldest Dwarf, "that those Northern Witches always mean the same thing, but in every age they have a different plan for getting it."

Chapter Sixteen

The Healing of Harms

WHEN JILL WOKE NEXT MORNING AND FOUND HER-
self in a cave, she thought for one horrid moment that she
was back in the Underworld. But when she noticed that
she was lying on a bed of heather with a furry mantle over
her, and saw a cheery fire crackling (as if newly lit) on a
stone hearth and, farther off, morning sunlight coming in
through the cave's mouth, she remembered all the happy
truth. They had had a delightful supper, all crowded into
that cave, in spite of being so sleepy before it was properly

over. She had a vague impression of Dwarfs crowding round the fire with frying-pans rather bigger than themselves, and the hissing, and delicious smell of sausages, and more, and more, and more sausages. And not wretched sausages half full of bread and soya bean either, but real meaty, spicy ones, fat and piping hot and burst and just the tiniest bit burnt. And great mugs of frothy chocolate, and roast potatoes and roast chestnuts, and baked apples with raisins stuck in where the cores had been, and then ices just to freshen you up after all the hot things.

Jill sat up and looked around. Puddleglum and Eustace were lying not far away, both fast asleep.

"Hi, you two!" shouted Jill in a loud voice. "Aren't you ever going to get up?"

"Shoo, shoo!" said a sleepy voice somewhere above her. "Time to be settling down. Have a good snooze, do, do. Don't make a to-do. Tu-whoo!"

"Why, I do believe," said Jill, glancing up at a white bundle of fluffy feathers which was perched on top of a grandfather clock in one corner of the cave, "I do believe it's Glimfeather!"

"True, true," whirred the Owl, lifting his head out from under his wing and opening one eye. "I came up with a message for the Prince at about two. The squirrels brought us the good news. Message for the Prince. He's gone. You're to follow too. Good-day—" and the head disappeared again.

As there seemed no further hope of getting any information from the Owl, Jill got up and began looking round for any chance of a wash and some breakfast. But almost at once a little Faun came trotting into the cave with a sharp click-clack of his goaty hoofs on the stone floor.

"Ah! You've woken up at last, Daughter of Eve," he said. "Perhaps you'd better wake the Son of Adam. You've got to be off in a few minutes and two Centaurs have very kindly offered to let you ride on their backs down to Cair Paravel." He added in a lower voice, "Of course, you realize it is a most special and unheard-of honor to be allowed to ride a Centaur. I don't know that I ever heard of anyone doing it before. It wouldn't do to keep them waiting."

"Where's the Prince?" was the first question of Eustace and Puddleglum as soon as they had been waked.

"He's gone down to meet the King, his father, at Cair Paravel," answered the Faun, whose name was Orruns. "His Majesty's ship is expected in harbor any moment. It seems that the King met Aslan—I don't know whether it was a vision or face to face—before he had sailed far, and Aslan turned him back and told him he would find his long-lost son awaiting him when he reached Narnia."

Eustace was now up and he and Jill set about helping Orruns to get the breakfast. Puddleglum was told to stay in bed. A Centaur called Cloudbirth, a famous healer, or (as Orruns called it) a "leech," was coming to see to his burnt foot.

"Ah!" said Puddleglum in a tone almost of content-ment, "he'll want to have the leg off at the knee, I shouldn't wonder. You see if he doesn't." But he was quite glad to stay in bed.

Breakfast was scrambled eggs and toast and Eustace tackled it just as if he had not had a very large supper in the middle of the night.

"I say, Son of Adam," said the Faun, looking with a cer-tain awe at Eustace's mouthfuls. "There's no need to hurry *quite* so dreadfully as that. I don't think the Centaurs have quite finished *their* breakfasts yet."

"Then they must have got up very late," said Eustace. "I bet it's after ten o'clock."

"Oh no," said Orruns. "They got up before it was light."

"Then they must have waited the dickens of a time for breakfast," said Eustace.

"No, they didn't," said Orruns. "They began eating the minute they awoke."

"Golly!" said Eustace. "Do they eat a very big breakfast?"

"Why, Son of Adam, don't you understand? A Centaur has a man-stomach and a horse-stomach. And of course both want breakfast. So first of all he has porridge and pavenders and kidneys and bacon and omelette and cold ham and toast and marmalade and coffee and beer. And after that he attends to the horse part of himself by grazing for an hour or so and finishing up with a hot mash, some oats, and a bag of sugar. That's why it's such a serious thing to ask a Centaur to stay for the weekend. A very serious thing indeed."

At that moment there was a sound of horse-hoofs tapping on rock from the mouth of the cave, and the children looked up. The two Centaurs, one with a black and one with a golden beard flowing over their magnificent bare chests, stood waiting for them, bending their heads a little so as to look into the cave. Then the children became very polite and finished their breakfast very quickly. No one thinks a Centaur funny when he sees it. They are solemn, majestic people, full of ancient wisdom which they learn from the stars, not easily made either merry or angry; but their anger is terrible as a tidal wave when it comes.

"Good-bye, dear Puddleglum," said Jill, going over to the Marsh-wiggle's bed. "I'm sorry we called you a wet blanket."

"So'm I," said Eustace. "You've been the best friend in the world."

"And I do hope we'll meet again," added Jill.

"Not much chance of that, I should say," replied Puddleglum. "I don't reckon I'm very likely to see my old wigwam again, either. And that Prince—he's a nice chap—but do you think he's very strong? Constitution ruined with living underground, I shouldn't wonder. Looks the sort that might go off any day."

"Puddleglum!" said Jill. "You're a regular old humbug. You sound as doleful as a funeral and I believe you're perfectly happy. And you talk as if you were afraid of everything, when you're really as brave as—as a lion."

"Now, speaking of funerals," began Puddleglum, but Jill, who heard the Centaurs tapping with their hoofs behind her, surprised him very much by flinging her arms round his thin neck and kissing his muddy-looking face, while Eustace wrung his hand. Then they both rushed away to the Centaurs, and the Marsh-wiggle, sinking back on his bed, remarked to himself, "Well, I wouldn't have dreamt of her doing that. Even though I *am* a good-looking chap."

To ride on a Centaur is, no doubt, a great honor (and except Jill and Eustace there is probably no one alive in the world today who has had it) but it is very uncomfortable. For no one who valued his life would suggest putting a saddle on a Centaur, and riding bare-back is no fun; especially if, like Eustace, you have never learned to ride at all. The Centaurs were very polite in a grave, gracious, grown-up kind of way, and as they cantered through the Narnian woods they spoke, without turning their heads, telling the children about the properties of herbs and roots, the influences of the planets, the nine names of Aslan with their meanings, and things of that sort. But however sore and jolted the two humans were, they would now give anything to have that journey over again: to see those glades and slopes sparkling with last night's snow, to be met by rabbits and squirrels and birds that wished you good morning, to breathe again the air of Narnia and hear the voices of the Narnian trees.

They came down to the river, flowing bright and blue in winter sunshine, far below the last bridge (which is at the snug, red-roofed little town of Beruna) and were ferried across in a flat barge by the ferryman; or rather, by the ferry-wiggle, for it is Marsh-wiggles who do most of the watery and fishy kinds of work in Narnia. And when they had crossed they rode along the south bank of the river and presently came to Cair Paravel itself. And at the very moment of their arrival they saw that same bright ship which they had seen when they first set foot in Narnia, gliding up the river like a huge bird. All the court were once more assembled on the green between the castle and the quay to welcome King Caspian home again. Rilian, who had changed his black clothes and was now dressed in a scarlet cloak over silver mail, stood close to the water's edge, bare-headed, to receive his father; and the Dwarf Trumpkin sat beside him in his little donkey-chair. The children saw there would be no chance of reaching the Prince through all that crowd, and, anyway, they now felt rather shy. So they asked the Centaurs if they might go on sitting on their backs a little longer and thus see everything over the heads of the courtiers. And the Centaurs said they might.

A flourish of silver trumpets came over the water from the ship's deck: the sailors threw a rope; rats (Talking Rats, of course) and Marsh-wiggles made it fast ashore; and the ship was warped in. Musicians, hidden somewhere in the crowd, began to play solemn, triumphal music. And soon the King's galleon was alongside and the Rats ran the gang-way on board her.

Jill expected to see the old King come down it. But there

appeared to be some hitch. A Lord with a pale face came ashore and knelt to the Prince and to Trumpkin. The three were talking with their heads close together for a few minutes, but no one could hear what they said. The music played on, but you could feel that everyone was becoming uneasy. Then four Knights, carrying something and going very slowly, appeared on deck. When they started to come down the gangway you could see what they were carrying: it was the old King on a bed, very pale and still. They set him down. The Prince knelt beside him and embraced him. They could see King Caspian raising his hand to bless his son. And everyone cheered, but it was a half-hearted cheer, for they all felt that something was going wrong. Then suddenly the King's head fell back upon his pillows, the musicians stopped and there was a dead silence. The Prince, kneeling by the King's bed, laid down his head upon it and wept.

There were whisperings and goings to and fro. Then Jill noticed that all who wore hats, bonnets, helmets, or hoods were taking them off—Eustace included. Then she heard a rustling and flapping noise up above the castle; when she looked she saw that the great banner with the golden Lion on it was being brought down to half-mast. And after that, slowly, mercilessly, with wailing strings and disconsolate blowing of horns, the music began again: this time, a tune to break your heart.

They both slipped off their Centaurs (who took no notice of them).

"I wish I was at home," said Jill.

Eustace nodded, saying nothing, and bit his lip.

"I have come," said a deep voice behind them. They turned and saw the Lion himself, so bright and real and strong that everything else began at once to look pale and shadowy compared with him. And in less time than it takes to breathe Jill forgot about the dead King of Narnia and remembered only how she had made Eustace fall over the cliff, and how she had helped to muff nearly all the signs, and about all the snappings and quarrelings. And she wanted to say "I'm sorry" but she could not speak. Then the Lion drew them toward him with his eyes, and bent down and touched their pale faces with his tongue, and said:

"Think of that no more. I will not always be scolding. You have done the work for which I sent you into Narnia."

"Please, Aslan," said Jill, "may we go home now?"

"Yes. I have come to bring you Home," said Aslan. Then he opened his mouth and blew. But this time they had no sense of flying through the air: instead, it seemed that they remained still, and the wild breath of Aslan blew away the ship and the dead King and the castle and the snow and the winter sky. For all these things floated off into the air like wreaths of smoke, and suddenly they were standing in a great brightness of mid-summer sunshine, on smooth turf, among mighty trees, and beside a fair, fresh stream. Then they saw that they were once more on the Mountain of Aslan, high up above and beyond the end of that world in which Narnia lies. But the strange thing was that the funeral music for King Caspian still went on, though no one could tell where it came from. They were walking beside the stream and the Lion went before them: and he became so beautiful, and the music so despairing, that Jill did not know which of them it was that filled her eyes with tears.

Then Aslan stopped, and the children looked into the stream. And there, on the golden gravel of the bed of the stream, lay King Caspian, dead, with the water flowing over him like liquid glass. His long white beard swayed in it like water-weed. And all three stood and wept. Even the Lion wept: great Lion-tears, each tear more precious than the Earth would be if it was a single solid diamond. And Jill noticed that Eustace looked neither like a child crying, nor like a boy crying and wanting to hide it, but like a grown-up crying. At least, that is the nearest she could get to it; but really, as she said, people don't seem to have any particular ages on that mountain.

"Son of Adam," said Aslan, "go into that thicket and pluck the thorn that you will find there, and bring it to me."

Eustace obeyed. The thorn was a foot long and sharp as a rapier.

"Drive it into my paw, Son of Adam," said Aslan, holding up his right fore-paw and spreading out the great pad toward Eustace.

"Must I?" said Eustace.

"Yes," said Aslan.

Then Eustace set his teeth and drove the thorn into the Lion's pad. And there came out a great drop of blood, redder than all redness that you have ever seen or imagined. And it splashed into the stream over the dead body of the King. At the same moment the doleful music stopped. And the dead King began to be changed. His white beard turned to gray, and from gray to yellow, and got shorter and vanished altogether; and his sunken cheeks grew round and fresh, and the wrinkles were smoothed, and his eyes opened, and his eyes and lips both laughed, and suddenly he leaped up and stood before them—a very young man, or a boy. (But Jill couldn't say which, because of people having no particular ages in Aslan's country. Even in this world, of course, it is the stupidest children who are the most childish and the stupidest grown-ups who are the most grown-up.) And he rushed to Aslan and flung his arms as far as they would go round the huge neck; and he gave Aslan the strong kisses of a King, and Aslan gave him the wild kisses of a Lion.

At last Caspian turned to the others. He gave a great laugh of astonished joy.

"Why! Eustace!" he said. "Eustace! So you did reach the end of the world after all. What about my second-best sword that you broke on the sea-serpent?"

Eustace made a step toward him with both hands held out, but then drew back with a startled expression.

"Look here! I say," he stammered. "It's all very well. But aren't you—? I mean, didn't you—?"

"Oh, don't be such an ass," said Caspian.

"But," said Eustace, looking at Aslan. "Hasn't he—er—died?"

"Yes," said the Lion in a very quiet voice, almost (Jill thought) as if he were laughing. "He has died. Most people have, you know. Even I have. There are very few who haven't."

"Oh," said Caspian. "I see what's bothering you. You think I'm a ghost, or some nonsense. But don't you see? I would be that if I appeared in Narnia now: because I don't belong there any more. But one can't be a ghost in one's own country. I might be a ghost if I got into your world. I don't know. But I suppose it isn't yours either, now you're here."

A great hope rose in the children's hearts. But Aslan shook his shaggy head. "No, my dears," he said. "When you meet me here again, you will have come to stay. But not now. You must go back to your own world for a while."

"Sir," said Caspian, "I've always wanted to have just one glimpse of *their* world. Is that wrong?"

"You cannot want wrong things any more, now that you have died, my son," said Aslan. "And you shall see their world—for five minutes of *their* time. It will take no longer for you to set things right there." Then Aslan explained to Caspian what Jill and Eustace were going back to and all about Experiment House: he seemed to know it quite as well as they did.

"Daughter," said Aslan to Jill, "pluck a switch off that bush." She did; and as soon as it was in her hand it turned into a fine new riding crop.

"Now, Sons of Adam, draw your swords," said Aslan. "But use only the flat, for it is cowards and children, not warriors, against whom I send you."

"Are you coming with us, Aslan?" said Jill.

"They shall see only my back," said Aslan.

He led them rapidly through the wood, and before they had gone many paces, the wall of Experiment House appeared before them. Then Aslan roared so that the sun shook in the sky and thirty feet of the wall fell down before them. They looked through the gap, down into the school shrubbery and on to the roof of the gym, all under the same dull autumn sky which they had seen before their adventures began. Aslan turned to Jill and Eustace and breathed upon them and touched their foreheads with his tongue. Then he lay down amid the gap he had made in the wall and turned his golden back to England, and his lordly face toward his own lands. At the same moment Jill saw figures whom she knew only too well running up through the laurels toward them. Most of the gang were there—Adela Pennyfather and Cholmondely Major, Edith Winterblott, "Spotty" Sorner, big Bannister, and the two loathsome Garrett twins. But suddenly they stopped. Their faces changed, and all the meanness, conceit, cruelty, and sneakishness almost disappeared in one single expression of terror. For they saw the wall fallen down, and a lion as large as a young elephant lying in the gap, and three figures in glittering clothes with weapons in their hands rushing down upon them. For, with the strength of Aslan in them, Jill plied her crop on the girls and Caspian and Eustace plied the flats of their swords on the boys so well that in two minutes all the bullies were running like mad, crying out, "Murder! Fascists! Lions! It isn't *fair*." And then the Head (who was, by the way, a woman) came running out to see what was happening. And when she saw the lion and the broken wall and Caspian and Jill and Eustace (whom she quite failed to recognize) she had hysterics and went back to the house and began ringing up the police with stories about a lion escaped from a circus, and escaped convicts who broke down walls and carried drawn swords. In the midst of all this fuss Jill and Eustace slipped quietly indoors and changed out of their bright clothes into ordinary things, and Caspian went back into his own world. And the wall, at Aslan's word, was made whole again. When the police arrived and found no lion, no broken wall, and no convicts, and the Head behaving like a lunatic, there was an inquiry into the whole thing.

And in the inquiry all sorts of things about Experiment House came out, and about ten people got expelled. After that, the Head's friends saw that the Head was no use as a Head, so they got her made an Inspector to interfere with other Heads. And when they found she wasn't much good even at that, they got her into Parliament where she lived happily ever after.

Eustace buried his fine clothes secretly one night in the school grounds, but Jill smuggled hers home and wore them at a fancy-dress ball next holidays. And from that day forth things changed for the better at Experiment House, and it became quite a good school. And Jill and Eustace were always friends.

But far off in Narnia, King Rilian buried his father, Caspian the Navigator, Tenth of that name, and mourned for him. He himself ruled Narnia well and the land was happy in his days, though Puddleglum (whose foot was as good as new in three weeks) often pointed out that bright mornings brought on wet afternoons, and that you couldn't expect good times to last. The opening into the hillside was left open, and often in hot summer days the Narnians go in there with ships and lanterns and down to the water and sail to and fro, singing, on the cool, dark underground sea, telling each other stories of the cities that lie fathoms deep below. If ever you have the luck to go to Narnia yourself, do not forget to have a look at those caves.

READ MORE   3

Chapter one from *The Last Battle*,
book seven in *The Chronicles of Narnia*

DISCOVER MORE   17

Excerpts from *Beyond the Wardrobe:
The Official Guide to Narnia*

DISCUSS MORE   30

Reading group guide to *The Silver Chair*

Bonus Excerpts and More!

Chapter One
from *The Last Battle*

By Caldron Pool

IN THE LAST DAYS OF NARNIA, FAR UP TO THE WEST beyond Lantern Waste and close beside the great waterfall, there lived an Ape. He was so old that no one could remember when he had first come to live in those parts, and he was the cleverest, ugliest, most wrinkled Ape you can imagine. He had a little house, built of wood and thatched with leaves, up in the fork of a great tree, and his name was Shift. There were very few Talking Beasts or Men or Dwarfs, or people of any sort, in that part of the wood, but Shift had one friend and neighbor who was a donkey called Puzzle. At least they both said they were friends, but from the way things went on you might have thought Puzzle was more like Shift's servant than his friend. He did all the work. When they went together to the river, Shift filled the big skin bottles with water but it was Puzzle who carried them back. When they wanted anything from the towns further down the river it was Puzzle who went down with empty panniers on his back and came back with the panniers full and heavy. And all the nicest things that Puzzle brought back were eaten by Shift; for as Shift said, "You see, Puzzle, I can't eat grass and thistles like you, so it's only fair I should make it up in other ways." And Puzzle always said, "Of course, Shift, of course. I see that." Puzzle never complained, because he knew that Shift was far cleverer than himself and he thought it was very kind of Shift to be friends with him at all. And if ever Puzzle did try to argue about anything, Shift would always say, "Now, Puzzle, I understand what needs to be done better than you. You know you're not clever, Puzzle." And Puzzle always said, "No, Shift. It's quite true. I'm *not* clever." Then he would sigh and do whatever Shift had said.

One morning early in the year the pair of them were out walking along the shore of Caldron Pool. Caldron Pool is the big pool right under the cliffs at the western end of Narnia. The great waterfall pours down into it with a noise like everlasting thunder, and the River of Narnia flows out on the other side. The waterfall keeps the Pool always dancing and bubbling and churning round and round as if it were on the boil, and that of course is how it got its name of Caldron Pool. It is liveliest in the early spring when the waterfall is swollen with all the snow that has melted off the mountains from up beyond Narnia in the Western Wild from which the river comes. And as they looked at Caldron Pool Shift suddenly pointed with his dark, skinny finger and said,

"Look! What's that?"

"What's what?" said Puzzle.

"That yellow thing that's just come down the waterfall. Look! There it is again, it's floating. We must find out what it is."

"Must we?" said Puzzle.

"Of course we must," said Shift. "It may be something useful. Just hop into the Pool like a good fellow and fish it out. Then we can have a proper look at it."

"Hop into the Pool?" said Puzzle, twitching his long ears.

"Well how are we to get it if you don't?" said the Ape.

"But—but," said Puzzle, "wouldn't it be better if *you* went in? Because, you see, it's you who wants to know what it is, and I don't much. And you've got hands, you see. You're as good as a Man or a Dwarf when it comes to catching hold of things. I've only got hoofs."

"Really, Puzzle," said Shift, "I didn't think you'd ever say a thing like that. I didn't think it of you, really."

"Why, what have I said wrong?" said the Ass, speaking in rather a humble voice, for he saw that Shift was very deeply offended. "All I meant was—"

"Wanting *me* to go into the water," said the Ape. "As if you didn't know perfectly well what weak chests Apes always have and how easily they catch cold! Very well. I *will* go in. I'm feeling cold enough already in this cruel wind. But I'll go in. I shall probably die. Then you'll be sorry."

And Shift's voice sounded as if he was just going to burst into tears.

"Please don't, please don't, please don't," said Puzzle, half braying, and half talking. "I never meant anything of the sort, Shift, really I didn't. You know how stupid I am and how I can't think of more than one thing at a time. I'd forgotten about your weak chest. Of course I'll go in. You mustn't think of doing it yourself. Promise me you won't, Shift."

So Shift promised, and Puzzle went cloppety-clop on his four hoofs round the rocky edge of the Pool to find a place where he could get in. Quite apart from the cold it was no joke getting into that quivering and foaming water, and Puzzle had to stand and shiver for a whole minute before he made up his mind to do it. But then Shift called out from behind him and said: "Perhaps I'd better do it after all, Puzzle." And when Puzzle heard that he said, "No, no. You promised. I'm in now," and in he went.

A great mass of foam got him in the face and filled his mouth with water and blinded him. Then he went under altogether for a few seconds, and when he came up again he was in quite another part of the Pool. Then the swirl caught him and carried him round and round and faster and faster till it took him right under the waterfall itself, and the force of the water plunged him down, deep down, so that he thought he would never be able to hold his breath till he came up again. And when he had come up and when at last he got somewhere near the thing he was trying to catch, it sailed away from him till it too got under the fall and was forced down to the bottom. When it came up again it was further from him than ever. But at last, when he was almost tired to death, and bruised all over and numb with cold, he succeeded in gripping the thing with his teeth. And out he came carrying it in front of him and getting his front hoofs tangled up in it, for it was as big as a large hearthrug, and it was very heavy and cold and slimy.

He flung it down in front of Shift and stood dripping and shivering and trying to get his breath back. But the Ape never looked at him or asked him how he felt. The Ape was too busy going round and round the Thing and spreading it out and patting it and smelling it. Then a wicked gleam came into his eye and he said:

"It is a lion's skin."

"Ee—auh—auh—oh, is it?" gasped Puzzle.

"Now I wonder . . . I wonder . . . I wonder," said Shift to himself, for he was thinking very hard.

"I wonder who killed the poor lion," said Puzzle presently. "It ought to be buried. We must have a funeral."

"Oh, it wasn't a Talking Lion," said Shift. "You needn't bother about *that*. There are no Talking Beasts up beyond the Falls, up in the Western Wild. This skin must have belonged to a dumb, wild lion."

This, by the way, was true. A Hunter, a Man, had killed and skinned this lion somewhere up in the Western Wild several months before. But that doesn't come into this story.

"All the same, Shift," said Puzzle, "even if the skin only belonged to a dumb, wild lion, oughtn't we to give it a decent burial? I mean, aren't all lions rather—well, rather solemn? Because of you know Who. Don't you see?"

"Don't you start getting ideas into your head, Puzzle," said Shift. "Because, you know, thinking isn't your strong point. We'll make this skin into a fine warm winter coat for you."

"Oh, I don't think I'd like that," said the Donkey. "It

would look—I mean, the other Beasts might think—that is to say, I shouldn't feel—"

"What are you talking about?" said Shift, scratching himself the wrong way up as Apes do.

"I don't think it would be respectful to the Great Lion, to Aslan himself, if an ass like me went about dressed up in a lion-skin," said Puzzle.

"Now don't stand arguing, please," said Shift. "What does an ass like you know about things of that sort? You know you're no good at thinking, Puzzle, so why don't you let me do your thinking for you? Why don't you treat me as I treat you? I don't think I can do everything. I know you're better at some things than I am. That's why I let you go into the Pool; I knew you'd do it better than me. But why can't I have my turn when it comes to something I *can* do and you can't? Am I never to be allowed to do anything? Do be fair. Turn and turn about."

"Oh, well, of course, if you put it that way," said Puzzle.

"I tell you what," said Shift. "You'd better take a good brisk trot down river as far as Chippingford and see if they have any oranges or bananas."

"But I'm so tired, Shift," pleaded Puzzle.

"Yes, but you are very cold and wet," said the Ape. "You want something to warm you up. A brisk trot would be just the thing. Besides, it's market day at Chippingford today." And then of course Puzzle said he would go.

As soon as he was alone Shift went shambling along, sometimes on two paws and sometimes on four, till he reached his own tree. Then he swung himself up from branch to branch, chattering and grinning all the time, and went into his little house. He found needle and thread and a big pair of scissors there; for he was a clever Ape and the Dwarfs had taught him how to sew. He put the ball of thread (it was very thick stuff, more like cord than thread) into his mouth so that his cheek bulged out as if he were sucking a big bit of toffee. He held the needle between his lips and took the scissors in his left paw. Then he came down the tree and shambled across to the lion-skin. He squatted down and got to work.

He saw at once that the body of the lion-skin would be too long for Puzzle and its neck too short. So he cut a good piece out of the body and used it to make a long collar for

Puzzle's long neck. Then he cut off the head and sewed the collar in between the head and the shoulders. He put threads on both sides of the skin so that it would tie up under Puzzle's chest and stomach. Every now and then a bird would pass overhead and Shift would stop his work, looking anxiously up. He did not want anyone to see what he was doing. But none of the birds he saw were Talking Birds, so it didn't matter.

Late in the afternoon Puzzle came back. He was not trotting but only plodding patiently along, the way donkeys do.

"There weren't any oranges," he said, "and there weren't any bananas. And I'm very tired." He lay down.

"Come and try on your beautiful new lion-skin coat," said Shift.

"Oh bother that old skin," said Puzzle. "I'll try it on in the morning. I'm too tired tonight."

"You *are* unkind, Puzzle," said Shift. "If *you're* tired what do you think I am? All day long, while you've been having a lovely refreshing walk down the valley, I've been working hard to make you a coat. My paws are so tired I can

hardly hold these scissors. And now you won't say thank
you—and you won't even look at the coat—and you don't
care—and—and—"

"My dear Shift," said Puzzle, getting up at once, "I am
so sorry. I've been horrid. Of course I'd love to try it on.
And it looks simply splendid. Do try it on me at once.
Please do."

"Well, stand still then," said the Ape. The skin was very
heavy for him to lift, but in the end, with a lot of pulling
and pushing and puffing and blowing, he got it onto the
donkey. He tied it underneath Puzzle's body and he tied
the legs to Puzzle's legs and the tail to Puzzle's tail. A good
deal of Puzzle's gray nose and face could be seen through
the open mouth of the lion's head. No one who had ever
seen a real lion would have been taken in for a moment.
But if someone who had never seen a lion looked at Puzzle
in his lion-skin he just might mistake him for a lion, if he
didn't come too close, and if the light was not too good,
and if Puzzle didn't let out a bray and didn't make any
noise with his hoofs.

"You look wonderful, wonderful," said the Ape. "If

anyone saw you now, they'd think you were Aslan, the Great Lion, himself."

"That would be dreadful," said Puzzle.

"No it wouldn't," said Shift. "Everyone would do whatever you told them."

"But I don't want to tell them anything."

"But you think of the good we could do!" said Shift. "You'd have me to advise you, you know. I'd think of sensible orders for you to give. And everyone would have to obey us, even the King himself. We would set everything right in Narnia."

"But isn't everything right already?" said Puzzle.

"What!" cried Shift. "Everything right—when there are no oranges or bananas?"

"Well, you know," said Puzzle, "there aren't many people—in fact, I don't think there's anyone but yourself—who wants those sort of things."

"There's sugar too," said Shift.

"H'm, yes," said the Ass. "It would be nice if there was more sugar."

"Well then, that's settled," said the Ape. "You will pretend to be Aslan, and I'll tell you what to say."

"No, no, no," said Puzzle. "Don't say such dreadful things. It would be wrong, Shift. I may be not very clever but I know that much. What would become of us if the real Aslan turned up?"

"I expect he'd be very pleased," said Shift. "Probably he sent us the lion-skin on purpose, so that we could set things to right. Anyway, he never *does* turn up, you know. Not nowadays."

At that moment there came a great thunderclap right overhead and the ground trembled with a small earthquake. Both the animals lost their balance and were flung on their faces.

"There!" gasped Puzzle, as soon as he had breath to speak. "It's a sign, a warning. I knew we were doing something dreadfully wicked. Take this wretched skin off me at once."

"No, no," said the Ape (whose mind worked very quickly). "It's a sign the other way. I was just going to say that if the real Aslan, as you call him, meant us to go on with this, he would send us a thunderclap and an earth-tremor.

It was just on the tip of my tongue, only the sign itself came before I could get the words out. You've *got* to do it now, Puzzle. And please don't let us have any more arguing. You know you don't understand these things. What could a donkey know about signs?"

Excerpts from
Beyond the Wardrobe:
The Official Guide
to Narnia

Getting There . . . and Back

The rule is simple: Traveling to Narnia requires an invitation.

Certainly there are exceptions, and many earthly people have traveled to Narnia accidentally through what Aslan calls "chinks or chasms between worlds." But such chinks are growing rarer, Aslan tells the Telmarines at the end of *Prince Caspian*, explaining how their ancestors fled into a cave on a South Pacific island and emerged on Narnia's world. That magical cave "was one of the last" of the chinks between worlds, Aslan says, although he adds, "I do not say *the* last."

It was, apparently, just such a combination of fate and magic that brought Digory and Polly to their first other-worldly destination in the Wood between the Worlds at the very beginning of *The Magician's Nephew*. Then the children simply chose a random pool to jump into as they attempted to elude the evil Jadis, and in this way they traveled to Narnia.

But under normal conditions, visitors must be called to Narnia. Even if it doesn't seem that way, they are pulled into Narnia only when needed. In *The Silver Chair*, Aslan tells Jill Pole that she and Eustace Scrubb must complete a task in Narnia. That is why "I called you and him here out of your own world," the Lion explains. Jill contradicts Aslan, saying, "[N]obody called me and Scrubb, you know. It was we who asked to come here." But Aslan replies, "You would not have called to me unless I had been calling to you."

Anyone who has visited Narnia is anxious to return. But it turns out that the traveler cannot control the voyage.

In *The Lion, the Witch and the Wardrobe*, wise Professor Kirke (who once was young Digory) tells the Pevensies, "Yes, of course you'll get back to Narnia again someday. Once a King in Narnia, always a King in Narnia. But don't go trying to use the same route twice. Indeed, don't *try* to get there at all. It'll happen when you're not looking for it."

Each of the stories in *The Chronicles* introduces a new, unanticipated way to get to Narnia and a new way for the characters to return home again.

The Silver Chair

Eustace is trying to cheer up his classmate Jill Pole, who is crying because the bullies at their school, Experiment House, won't leave her alone. Explaining why he has changed so dramatically since the last school term, Eustace tells Jill about his strange experiences in Narnia. Even though Jill doesn't quite believe Eustace's stories, she says she would like to go to Narnia. To avoid the bullies, they run through the schoolyard and discover that the door in a stone wall is unlocked. Passing through the doorway, they find themselves on a cliff high above Narnia.

After they complete an important mission for Aslan, they follow him through the Narnian woods until they are suddenly back on the familiar school property on Earth, right in front of the stone wall again. But Aslan is with them and brings along King Caspian, who has been resurrected from death by the Lion and appears to be a very young man. Aslan roars and the stone wall at Experiment House falls, revealing seven of the school bullies running to attack Jill and Eustace. But when the bullies see an enormous lion through the gap in the wall, they stop, terribly frightened. And the next thing they know, three armed figures in exquisite clothing—Caspian, Eustace and Jill— are beating them with a switch and the flats of swords. Aslan and Caspian, the only Narnian ever to visit Earth, remain on this world for only five minutes, but it is sufficient to change Experiment House and the bullies forever.

*

Good Characters in The Silver Chair

Lewis wrote that Eustace Clarence Scrubb almost deserved his name, which gives a clear indication of the Pevensie cousin's unpleasant personality. At nine years of age in

The Voyage of the Dawn Treader, Eustace is surly, disagreeable and a bully. Worst of all, as Lewis points out, he has no imagination. From the start, he hates being stuck in Narnia and wants to go home. As with many of Lewis's young characters, though, transformation is possible for Eustace. After he is unwittingly turned into a dragon, he finally understands the need for friendship and becomes a much nicer person (although he still complains occasionally). Later on Earth, at Experiment House, he shows real concern for Jill, who is being pursued by the school bullies. When he is sent back to Narnia in *The Silver Chair*, and later in *The Last Battle*, Eustace proves himself a loyal, brave and capable boy.

Jill Pole is a classmate of Eustace and hates Experiment House even more than he does. While she is a smart girl, Jill is very angry and a bit stuck-up when we meet her in *The Silver Chair*. During her time in Narnia, she is humbled and grows to be more understanding. She also bravely plays her part in rescuing Prince Rilian. In *The Last Battle*, when she is a few years older, Jill's bravery and quick think-

ing go a long way toward helping the King fight the ulti-
mately losing battle. Lewis may have taken the name *Jill*
from one of the students who stayed with him during the
air raids of World War II, Jill Flewett. That Jill grew up to
be an actress and married the grandson of Sigmund Freud.
She and Lewis kept in touch for many years.

Glimfeather is an enormous, white-feathered Talking
Owl, as tall as a "good-sized dwarf," who flies Jill Pole to the
parliament of owls in *The Silver Chair*. (In giving the owls a
parliamentary organization, Lewis seems to offer a
humorous poke at "The Parliament of Fowls," a poem by
Geoffrey Chaucer. But he also using the little-known term
for a group or flock of owls, which is a "parliament.")
When Glimfeather first appears, he seems a bit befuddled
and comical. Like his fellow owls, he speaks partly in
rhyme. "Whoo! Tu-whoo! What a to-do! I can't think
clearly yet. It's too early," he tells Eustace and Jill. But after
nightfall, the nocturnal owl is very businesslike, issuing
instructions to the children that he clearly expects to be
obeyed. He also proves to be honest, blunt and loyal to the
king, all of which prove important in helping the children

to execute the mission that Aslan has set for them: find the missing Prince Rilian.

Puddleglum the Marsh-wiggle has a tall, skinny body, webbed hands and feet like a frog and "greeny-gray" hair, the strands of which are flat, not round—more like reeds than like human hair. Marsh-wiggles are one with the watery, reedy, muddy marshes north of Cair Paravel where they live in wigwams and fish for eels with long poles and lines. They are as fond of their privacy as eel stew, eel pie and fricasseed frogs. After dinner, they like to smoke pipes filled with their favorite heavy, muddy tobacco. Puddleglum, like all Marsh-wiggles, is philosophical and pessimistic, expecting the worst in every situation. When he first greets Eustace and Jill in *The Silver Chair*, Puddleglum says, "Good morning, Guests. Though when I say *good* I don't mean it won't probably turn to rain or it might be snow, or fog, or thunder." Although he serves as the book's comic relief, he is also brave and has good sense, which is why he is chosen to assist Eustace and Jill in their quest to save Prince Rilian. More important, Puddleglum possesses unshakable faith in the power of good. He is prepared to believe in goodness whether it exists or not, simply because it is the right thing in which to believe. It is Puddleglum's faith that breaks the Queen of Underland's enchantment of him and his companions, making it possible for them to rescue Prince Rilian and return to the world's surface. As Lewis's stepson Douglas Gresham reports: "Many of the characters [in Narnia] were drawn from people living in and around The Kilns [Lewis's longtime home]. The classic example of this is Puddleglum the Marsh-wiggle, a direct modeling of our gardener, Fred Paxford." In his book *Lenten Lands*, Gresham recounts a conversation with Paxford to illustrate the gardener's somewhat pessimistic outlook: "'Good morning, Fred,' I might say. 'Ah, looks loike rain afore lunch though, if'n it doan't snow.'" So it can be seen as a homage to Paxford when, at the conclusion of *The Silver Chair*, Lewis writes that Narnia was happy under King Rilian, but that Puddleglum "often pointed out that bright mornings brought on wet afternoons, and that you couldn't expect good times to last."

Rilian is the son of King Caspian and Ramandu's daughter. When his mother is killed by a huge green serpent at the beginning of *The Silver Chair*, Prince Rilian sets off to find the snake and avenge her murder. Before his mother's death, Rilian was a charming and carefree young knight who loved to laugh and tell stories with his friends. But after her death, his search for the snake leaves him "tired and distraught," as one of the owls tells Eustace and Jill. Rilian is bewitched by a beautiful woman, who calls herself the Queen of Underland or the Lady of the Green Kirtle. Also known as the green Witch, it turns out that she is able to transform herself into a deadly green snake. She enslaves the Prince in her underground kingdom, making him forget his former life on the surface. He remembers his true identity for only one hour a day, but the green Witch keeps him strapped into a magical silver chair during that hour so he cannot escape. Once Rilian is rescued by Eustace, Jill and Puddleglum, he fights bravely to free them all from the wicked Witch and to avenge his mother's murder. He goes on to rule Narnia after his father's death. Fair and honest, Rilian "ruled Narnia well and the land was happy in his days...."

Bad Creatures *in* The Silver Chair

The Bad Giants of Narnia. There are a few races of bad
giants, and they all live in the North of Narnia. The "gentle
giants" of Harfang are described as gentle only by the lying
Lady of the Green Kirtle. Though these giants may seem
gentle on the outside as they welcome Puddleglum, Jill and
Eustace to their large home, they show their true colors
when Jill discovers their plan to eat the visitors at their
Autumn Feast. There are even fiercer giants further north,
whom Peter, and later Caspian, vanquish. And yet a third
race, called the Ettins, fight alongside the White Witch
against Aslan.

The Lady of the Green Kirtle, who also calls herself
Queen of Underland or Queen of the Deep Realm,
appears only in *The Silver Chair*. Many who know her
refer to her as the green Witch. She is very beautiful, with a
lovely musical laugh. She has the power to make people
forget their old lives and their identities along with their
most deeply held beliefs. She can also transform herself
into a deadly green serpent, which is how she murders the

Queen of Narnia, King Caspian's wife and Prince Rilian's mother. The green Witch later enchants Rilian, trapping him in Underland where she has control over all the peoples who live beneath Narnia's surface. In her serpent form, the green Witch tries to kill Rilian, but instead, Rilian, Puddleglum, Eustace and Jill destroy *her* and free the rest of the underworld's slaves from her evil spell.

*

A Marsh-wiggle Proves the Power of Faith

As the battle to overcome evil in Narnia continues, *The Silver Chair* is a tale about the paramount importance of trust and faith, without which the children and Rilian would have been lost forever in the pit of Underland. It is a lack of trust in both Aslan and themselves that causes Jill and Eustace to miss Aslan's signs. They don't understand the signs and have little faith that they will recognize them. So they don't. As the story progresses, their trust in each other grows and, with it, their ability to recognize Aslan's signs and to see reality clearly.

In the end, it is Puddleglum's faith in goodness that breaks the Witch-queen's evil, enchanted hold on him and his companions. The Witch has cast a spell on Puddleglum, Jill, Eustace and Rilian by sprinkling a green powder into the fire in her fireplace. The burning powder fills the room with a sweet-smelling smoke that dulls the captives' minds. With the enchanted smoke's help, the Witch succeeds in making the four believe that Narnia and Aslan don't really exist and that the sun and the stars are delusions.

But Puddleglum manages to shake off the spell long enough to bravely stamp out the fire with his bare, webbed foot, inflicting considerable pain on himself. His sacrifice works. With the fire nearly out, the enchanted smoke dissipates and the pain itself clears the Marsh-wiggle's head. Suddenly "he knew exactly what he really thought." In this clearheaded instant, Puddleglum concludes that what the Witch is saying doesn't matter because both the Lion and the land stand for goodness—and Puddleglum has faith in the power and the rightness of good.

"Suppose we *have* only dreamed, or made up, all those things—trees and grass and sun and moon and stars and Aslan himself.... Then all I can say is that, in that case, the

made-up things seem a good deal more important than
the real ones. . . . I'm on Aslan's side even if there isn't any
Aslan to lead it," Puddleglum tells Underland's queen.
And the spell is broken by the Marsh-wiggle's faith and
courage.

Reading
Group Guide

ABOUT THE CHRONICLES OF NARNIA

The Lion, the Witch and the Wardrobe was first published in 1950, but C. S. Lewis began piecing together the story long before that. The tales and ancient myths his Irish nurse told always fascinated him, and when he was sixteen, a picture of a faun carrying parcels and an umbrella in the snowy woods popped into his head. Years later, during World War II, four children stayed with Mr. Lewis at his country house and stirred his imagination again. Not long afterward, he began writing the story that would become

The Lion, the Witch and the Wardrobe.

After being illustrated by Pauline Baynes, *The Lion, the Witch and the Wardrobe* was published to great success. With so many stories to tell about Narnia and its unforgettable characters, Lewis wrote six more books. Published in 1956, *The Last Battle* was awarded the Carnegie Medal— England's highest honor for children's literature.

More than eighty-five million readers worldwide have discovered *The Chronicles of Narnia*. As you read the books for the first time, or rediscover their magic, take some time to discuss them. The following questions and topics are intended to spark debate about subjects such as good versus evil, symbolism and relationships. So gather round and journey once more to the wondrous land of Narnia.

BOOK SIX
THE SILVER CHAIR

"'Pole, I say, are you good at believing things? I mean things that everyone here would laugh at?'

"'I've never had the chance,' said Jill, 'but I think I would be'" (p. 5).

Questions for Group Discussion

1. Much of the novel is spent in bleaker lands than Narnia. Other than physical characteristics, what are some differences? Are any of the inhabitants at all similar to Narnians?

2. How do Puddleglum's actions contrast with his attitudes? Does he do anything surprising? Can he be characterized as a hero? Can Jill or Eustace, given their behavior?

3. Jill and Eustace are misled by the appearance of the Queen of Underland and the festival at Harfang. At what other times are they deceived by appearances?

4. What do you think of the way Aslan behaves toward Jill when she first encounters him by the river? What is he trying to get her to learn, or to acknowledge?

5. Look for places where stories are told within the story. How do you feel the "story within a story" device is used to slow down or speed up the story, to show different points of view and to get information across? How does the credibility of the speaker affect the way we receive the information?

6. Find examples of times when characters act unafraid

although they really are afraid. When is this a foolish thing to do? When is it necessary?

7. How does Jill use expected "girlish" behavior to get what she really wants from the Giants? How can people use other people's mistaken expectations of them to their own advantage?

8. Why does the Witch try to enchant the characters into believing there is no Overworld? For what might this be an allegory?

9. How do the children finally get revenge on the bullies at school in their own world? Do you find this to be a satisfying ending? Why or why not?

10. Since Aslan knows all that is to come, he must know that Jill will miss some of the signs. If that's true, why do you think he gives them to her? Why do you think he sends the children on this quest rather than simply freeing the Prince himself? Can you think of times where it was important to learn through experiencing something yourself rather than being shown or told? What are some of the difficulties that arise in allowing someone you care about to learn through experience?

What Would You Do?

The Knight makes the children promise not to cut the cords no matter what he says. Then when his "enchantment" comes upon him, he reverses his argument. "It is at this hour that I am in my right mind: it is all the rest of the day that I am enchanted." How should the children know which to believe?

Discuss Quotes

What do the following quotes mean in context? What do you think of the ideas expressed?

"You have seen lamps, and so you imagined a bigger and better lamp and called it the *sun*. You've seen cats, and now you want a bigger and better cat, and it's to be called a *lion*" (the Witch, p. 194).

"Friends . . . when once a man is launched on such an adventure as this, he must bid farewell to hopes and fears, otherwise death or deliverance will both come too late to save his honor and his reason" (Prince Rilian, p. 209).

DISCUSSIONS ACROSS
THE CHRONICLES OF NARNIA

The following questions are designed to spark discussion about the issues and topics raised across the series.

Childhood and Adulthood

"Children have one kind of silliness, as you know, and grown-ups have another kind" (*The Magician's Nephew*, p. 88). How would you describe the difference between these kinds of silliness? What are some other observations the author makes about children and adults? Do you think Lewis remembered his own childhood or had a sense of how children think? Why or why not?

Complexity of Emotion

Lewis frequently shows characters feeling more than one thing at once, or experiencing closely alternating emotions. Find examples of this in the books and see if you can explain the characters' experience. Can you think of a time when you felt two different ways about something in your own life?

Gender Roles

Compare male and female roles in the books. How do the Narnia chronicles reflect different expectations for boys and girls? How do attitudes about gender roles at the time the series was written (early to mid-1950s) compare with attitudes now?

Recurring Characters

Why do you think the author decides to send particular characters—and not others—on each specific voyage?

Talking and Nontalking Beasts

What distinction is made between Talking Beasts and nontalking beasts? Why do Narnians consider it horrible to kill or eat a Talking Beast when it is okay to kill or eat a nontalking one? What does this say about the importance of speech to the author, or as an attribute of humanity?

THEMES
Beliefs

Characters regularly confront issues of good and evil. How does what a character believes affect how he or she acts and vice versa? What are some examples of good and evil behavior? How do the characters respond to good and evil?

Courage

When do characters show courage? Examine the difference between rash action and courageous action. What is the difference between caution and cowardice? How does fear affect how the characters perceive the world, and how they act?

Fantasy

What are the elements that make up fantasy? What images of this fantasy world are most vivid? How do the children adapt to the altered realities of Narnia? What preconceptions do they bring with them?